Delusions

by Stuart Rawlings

Sierra Dreams Press

Published by Sierra Dreams Press
15200 Wild Oak Lane, Auburn, CA 95603
(530) 878-8831
www.sierradreamspress.com
stuartrawlings@hughes.net

First Edition 2012
Second Edition 2019
Also available in eBook and Audiobook formats
ISBN-13: 978-0-9771405-3-4

Cover and chapter art by Jane Roach
Proofread by Madonna Anglin
Second Edition typeset by VivoCreative.Group

Preface

When I was ten years old and living in San Francisco, my mother, Kay, was a film producer for KQED-TV, San Francisco's new educational station. Her first big show was Captain Zero, about a spaceman who had a time machine which he used to travel back in time and visit famous people of the past. One day my mother came to me and said, "Stuart, how would you like to be in one of my episodes? You would be playing the part of the son of William Tell, the famous Swiss crossbow marksman."

I said "Yes," because one never said no to my mother. Two weeks later, I appeared on the set of a rural scene in "medieval Switzerland," dressed in the costume of a peasant boy. I had few lines, and discovered to my horror that my main contribution to the show was to have an apple shot off my head from thirty feet by an arrow from an 80-lb. crossbow.

To make it short, the arrow missed my head and pierced the apple above me—before passing through the tree and two adjacent studio walls, and settling into the back of a wooden chair. All was well, and I never forgot the name of William Tell.

My interest in history continued as I became a devoted admirer of H.G. Wells, the British science fiction writer of the early 1900s. My favorite story of his was *The Time Machine*, in which a scientist develops a contraption similar to the one used by Captain Zero to visit famous people in times past. As my interest in history grew, I found myself wishing that I, too, had one of these machines. The person I most wanted to meet was Jesus, although Buddha, Thomas Jefferson, and H.G. Wells himself were not far behind.

In October of 2008, I knew that there was very little

possibility that the foremost scientists of my era were likely to develop such a time machine during the remainder of my lifetime. But then again, I knew that as a science fiction writer, my imagination had no such limits. I could create anything or anyone I wanted to in my mind. Yes, I could meet any and all of the people on my list. Not only that, I could interact with them, ask them questions, and be asked questions in return. I could experience them in different moods and circumstances. It could be in their time and place, or mine, or maybe some other time and place. Anything.

One day that month, while a social worker at a mental health residential treatment facility in Roseville, California, I had a conceptual breakthrough. I decided to place my cherished historical characters in that particular mental heath facility, as patients, entering one by one. They could each roughly resemble their namesakes, and they could interact with me, the staff, and each other, in a semi-plausible setting.

That night, at my home in Auburn, I opened a folder called *Delusions* and started to write. As with my last novel (*Another Messiah*, 2005), the words came flowing out, although this time the writing took not two months, but three years. Unlike my last novel, this time I felt no delusions about this project ever bringing me fame or fortune. No, this one was being written just for me and a handful of like-minded eccentric friends.

Before continuing, I need to issue a warning. This book is by far the most provocative of any of the twenty-two books I have written to date. It may offend traditional Christians, Jews, Moslems and conservative Americans. If you happen to fall within any of these categories, then I suggest that you close this book now and forever.

For everyone else, let me invite you into Stuart's little fantasy world—where some of the most fascinating people in history are alive and well, and where there are no limits to the imagination.

— Stuart Rawlings
Auburn, California
September 1, 2012

Contents

CHAPTER ONE

Rosewood

Halloween decorations were up at Rosewood, the mental health facility where I worked. There were carved pumpkins with crooked teeth, figures of witches on broomsticks, spiders hanging from ceilings, and paintings of Frankenstein and a headless horseman beneath a full moon on a window looking out on the patio.

But the scariest part of Rosewood was the faces of the staff. It had been two full weeks since we'd had any patients at all at our twelve-bed facility, and we were worried about losing our jobs. Housing prices were in free-fall, the stock market was down 30% in the last month, and predictions for the future ranged from short-term gloomy to long-term gloomy. This was no time to be unemployed.

Given all this, there was nothing less than jubilation when a phone call came from a nearby hospital at 8:33 a.m., informing us that a new patient would be arriving later that day. We didn't care who it was—what gender, age, or diagnosis. We were happy to have someone to work with again, to have hope that maybe we wouldn't be laid off, and to feel more secure about paying for food for our families, gas for our cars, and rent to shelter our families from the cold.

Most of the clients at Rosewood had mental health disorders such as schizophrenia, bipolar, or severe depression. My job was to meet with the clients, to talk to them individually and in groups, and to inspire, motivate, entertain, and fill them with positive energy as best as possible. I generally liked the work because I liked the clients, the staff around me, and the Director of Rosewood, whom I considered to be an Angel.

Perhaps I should mention here that I have long seen the world as containing three kinds of people: Angels, Dragons, and everyone else. In Glacier County Mental Health, there were a lot of Angels in the lower echelons of the work, while the top management was full of Dragons. But more about that later.

There were twelve patient beds at Rosewood, and the premises consisted of a main office, three smaller offices, a dining area, kitchen, outside patio, TV room, and six double-occupancy

2

bedrooms (each with a bathroom) along a hallway. There was also a "Quiet Room," where patients were taken when they became severely psychotic or unruly. In this room, clients might be restrained or given shots to calm them down. The truth is that when used, this room was anything but quiet.

Our patients generally came to us from one of California's transitional psychiatric hospitals after exhibiting 5150 tendencies—what the State of California called a "danger to self, danger to others, or grave disability due to a mental illness." Some of our patients were cutters or burners. Usually they did this to their wrists or arms with some sharp instrument or cigarettes, to gain attention. Others had dangerous behaviors, such as walking into fast-moving traffic or trying to jump off of high bridges. Others tended to look outside themselves to express their feelings—like picking fights with others or trying to kill them. Still others had thought disorders in which they couldn't quite relate to normal linear patterns. For example, if asked "What's your name?" the patient might answer, "Did Uncle Henry send you to torment me because of what I did to him when I was four? And by the way, what's for dinner?" Almost all the patients were delusional in some way, so their notion of reality was different than it was for the rest of us.

*****

Before we continue, a few words about me. The name's Patrick O'Leary, but I've never related much to my Irish ancestry. My father, Sean, used to boast how earlier generations of O'Learys had fought just about everybody who came to visit: first the Vikings, then the Normans (or French), and then the Protestant English (Henry VIII, Elizabeth I, and so on). But this fighting pride eventually got him in trouble. When I was fifteen, he started a brawl with another Irishman in a pub on St. Patrick's Day, and ended up dying from a whiskey bottle delivered to his head.

Since then, I've shed the mantle of Irish culture, or any kind of nationalism, and have gone my own way around the world in search of adventure. I spent six months in Peru, a year in Europe, another in Africa, and another in South Asia, followed by several trips to remote areas of the Amazon Basin. It doesn't really matter what I did in these places. As I see it, the important thing is that no matter where I am, when I get up in the morning, my mind often drifts off to somewhere far away, or to someone unusual whom I met in the course of my travels. And then I return to the present and wonder, "Who am I?" and "What am I doing here?"

So how did I get to this relatively mundane job at Rosewood, in the California foothills? Well, in the course of my travels, I slept with a woman called Rosie, who gave birth later to a baby girl. Mother and child moved here to Auburn, but I never knew any of this until one night when I got a call while I was in the Australian outback.

"Hey Patrick," Rosie said, "Guess what!"

"What?" I answered meekly, amazed that she had found me.

"Well, you're the father of a beautiful baby girl called Brigit. And guess what else."

"What?" I said, my mind spinning from what I'd just heard.

"Well, I've only got a few weeks to live, and you're gonna have to take responsibility for what you've done. So get your ass over here!"

Within a few weeks, Rosie had died, and I'd moved half a planet away to Auburn, California, where I was trying to father this truly beautiful little creature while working at the Rosewood Psychiatric Facility.

But enough about me.

*****

When the phone call came in at 8:33 on a Monday morning, telling staff that we had a new patient, we wrote down his first name and first initial of the last name on our board, according to protocol: "Adolph H." One hour later, we received a fax with

4

this discharge summary:

PATIENT: *Adolph Hitler (aliases Johann Schroeder, Hans Von Grumman, Rolphe Schmittenmeister, Martin Schindler, and Ludwig Neiderhofer)*

RECENT HISTORY: *Patient is a white male, 5'6" tall, weighing 135 pounds, and appearing to be in his mid-eighties. He was found in the shed of a back yard in Newcastle, California, suffering from a lack of shelter and food, and from hypothermia. When police officers obtained a German translator and tried to give assistance, he refused to cooperate. He was then 5150ed as gravely disabled and taken to Sutter Roseville Hospital. After being medically cleared, he was sent to the Rosewood Psychiatric Facility.*

Patient stated that he wanted no help from "Jewish pigs," although he did accept some food and a place to sleep. His frequent bursts of anger appeared to be directed toward everyone in his proximity, including doctors, nurses, social workers and German translators. Although he has not yet physically attacked anyone, his rhetoric and uncontrolled outbursts suggest that he has a potential for violence.

BACKGROUND: *Patient claims to have been born on April 20, 1889, in a town called Braunan Am Inn in Austria-Hungary. He claims to have had a troubled childhood, to have failed as a sketch artist, to have been wounded in the trenches of World War I, and to have risen to power to become the Chancellor of Germany from 1933 to 1945. He reports that he was briefly married to a woman called Eva Braun, shortly before they both tried to commit suicide in a Berlin bunker. She was "successful," but he was not. Since then, he reports to have been hiding, mostly in South America, with much of the rest of the world trying to find and kill him. No other family was mentioned, and all friends were reported to be either dead or in hiding.*

MEDICAL HISTORY: *History of syphilis, Parkinson's disease, poor dental health, and irregular eating habits with excessive amounts of sugar. Also reports of severe stomach cramps, insomnia and eczema, possibly caused by a vegetarian diet*

PSYCHIATRIC DIAGNOSES: *Schizophrenia, paranoid type; intermittent explosive disorder; post traumatic stress disorder; adult antisocial behavior; and lack of support from family or friends.*

As we sat in the office discussing this new case, our tone changed from jocular to serious, especially as two of our staff were Jewish. We were interested to see if Adolph looked like the Hitler we had seen in documentary movies, if his speech and manner had some of the powerful energy of the well-known dictator, and if he would relate at all to an American, or "enemy" staff. We discussed whether or not we should "play the game" with him—to treat him like der Fuehrer, or to speak to him openly about this being a delusion. The decision was made to play this by ear. We would pretend that he was who he said he was for a while, and then, at some point, bring him back to reality, whatever that might be.

CHAPTER TWO

Adolph H.

Around 3:15 p.m., one female social worker and one large male German translator, both white, escorted a short, elderly, pale, thin man through the front door of our Rosewood facility. He had on a worn grey suit with elbow patches, a faded white shirt, and black shoes. His receding hair was long and white, and there was no sign of the signature chopped moustache of his namesake. His skeletal body appeared tired as he leaned against a desk, and his beady eyes were cast down at the floor, making contact with no one.

My first feeling was one of pity. He seemed totally out of place, which I suppose would have been the case had the real Adolph Hitler just walked through the door. He was trying to shut us out as best as possible, as Nicholas, our Angel-in-Chief, gave him the traditional welcome speech, waiting calmly after each sentence for the translation into German:

"Adolph, welcome to Rosewood. (pause) This is an acute psychiatric treatment facility, which we will try to make as comfortable as possible for you. (pause) We hope that you will work with our doctors on appropriate medications (pause), and with our staff to develop a plan to help you improve your life."

The tone of Nicholas' voice was as sweet as can be, but there was no visible indication from Adolph that he was paying the slightest attention. Nicholas continued, "Adolph, I'd like to introduce you to our staff. (pause) My name is Nicholas, and I'm the Director of Rosewood. (pause) This is Tawny, who's in charge of medications." (Tawny was a nice woman of around forty, who was looking for a husband if she could ever take the risk of trusting men again.) "This is Scott, who's in charge of scheduling." (Scott was an accomplished guitarist and aspiring playwright.) "This is Amy, who takes care of meals and supplies." (Amy was a former military nurse and a no-nonsense social worker.) "This is Patrick, a social worker." (I felt like I was much more than that, but it didn't need elaboration at this time.) "And this is Sarah, a social work intern." (Sarah was a petite young African American woman, barely out of college.)

Faster than the eye could follow, our new client leaped at

Sarah and started to strangle her. And almost as fast, Scott and I grabbed the arms of the old man and held him in our newly-taught position of restraint. Scott and I soon had one of our feet and legs in front of Adolph, his arms held securely behind him, his head down, and his body in a position of helpless imbalance.

After checking to see if Sarah was all right (which she was), Nicholas said in a cool manner, "Now Adolph, we're going to take you to the Quiet Room to help you settle down." (pause for translation) "I know this is difficult for you (pause), but we'll try our best to make you feel comfortable in your new home here at Rosewood."

Scott and I kept holding Adolph's arms as we walked through a hall of faux spiders and cobwebs, and into the QR, where there was a bed in the middle of the room, and nothing else. When we loosened our grip, Adolph began struggling, so we were forced to get help and tie him down to the bed on his back, with straps around each foot, each arm, and his chest. Soon Dr. Jablonski, a Jewish psychiatrist from Poland, came in and gave him a shot of morpholine, which put him to sleep.

For the next two hours, my job was to attend Adolph in the QR. My mind was a swirl of thoughts and emotions as I tried to make sense of what was happening. Here was a person who, regardless of reality, seemingly believed that he was the most despised tyrant in all history—the one responsible for the execution of over 14 million innocent people, and of 6 million Jews—not to mention the 60 million or so others who had died in a senseless war.

I looked carefully at the form in front of me. His eyes were closed, his body limp on the white sheets of the bed. There was a scar on his left cheek—Lord knows where that came from. His face was pale to the point of ashen, and his face and hands had the liver spots of a man who was moving on in age. His white beard was thin, like those of elder Vietnamese men I had met in Saigon during the 1968 Tet Offensive. His eyebrows still had a trace of black, and yes, there was some resemblance in his nose, lips and chin to the historic figure I had seen in photographs. As

I watched him sleep, I thought about how, at this unconscious point in time, he was no different than the seven billion other people living on this planet we call Earth.

Why had he attacked Sarah? Because she was black? Because she was young, small, and vulnerable? Because she was closest to him at the time? For some other reason, or no reason? He'd evidenced no thought process before the assault. It was as if his body was reacting to a directive made by some remote, instinctive force over which he had no control. Was this man inhabited by demons? Did he have a rational mind? Was he human?

It was this last question that occupied my mind for the next hour, both in terms of the man in front of me and the terrible dictator of recent history, which, as far as I was concerned at this point in time, were the same. For most people, the name Hitler epitomized the vilest form of life, the darkest side of humanity, and the essence of evil. And yet, as far as we knew, this man was also human. Did he not experience joy, sadness and depression, the same as the rest of us? Did he not have love somewhere in his heart? Did he have some kind of conscience, no matter how small? And if he did, how could he reconcile his behavior of causing the deaths of so many millions of innocent people with this conscience? Did he feel any remorse at all for what he had done?

My mind moved on to the question of how I would feel if I believed I were Hitler—living in a world which despised me and would likely kill me in a second if my identity were suddenly revealed and the opportunity arose. How would it feel to be responsible for the Holocaust? As a social worker, I imagined this to be the most extreme form of paranoia imaginable. And, of course, I would want to help this person, regardless of whether or not this belief was founded in reality.

For two hours, the thin grey-suited man before me slept on the white-sheeted mattress. When, at last, he awoke, he was led, eyes ever downward, to a room at the end of the hall. He stayed there in his bed and slept through the night.

When I came to work the next morning, I found him eating a breakfast of scrambled eggs and bacon cooked by one of our staff. He looked more rested, but there was no hint of a desire to communicate with anyone on any level. When I said, "Good morning, Adolph. *Gutentag,*" there was no response. When it came time for his medications, he refused them with a shake of his head and walked back to his room, where he spent the rest of the day. Another German translator who came later that day found a similar lack of response to all questions.

The truth was that during the first three days of his stay with us, Adolph did nothing but eat, sleep, shower, dress, undress, and go to the bathroom. I began to think that this fascinating creature would never, ever, reveal any of the mysteries that lay within.

*****

On the morning of the third day after Adolph's arrival, there was another phone call from a local hospital. This one also evoked great excitement from our staff, for we were still desperate for patients and longed to have someone we could actually work with in terms of mental health treatment. This is the fax we received one hour later:

PATIENT: *Jesus Christ*

RECENT HISTORY: *Patient is a dark-skinned male, 6 feet tall, weighing 155 pounds, and appearing to be in his mid-30s. He was found on a rainy night outside a camp inhabited by homeless people. When he evidenced no interest in applying for aid himself, or in accepting a coat to protect against the rain, the police were called. They reported that he appeared to be hallucinating, and was unable to respond to their persistent questions about who he was and how he might survive the stormy night. They 5150ed him as gravely disabled and took him to the Sutter Roseville Hospital, where he was medically cleared and sent to*

11

the Rosewood Psychiatric Facility.

BACKGROUND: *Client reported to a hospital social worker that he believed he had been born twice, and had lived two separate lives. The first birth was two thousand years ago in Bethlehem, at that time part of the Roman Empire. He claims to have had an unremarkable childhood in Nazareth near the Sea of Galilee, although his relationship with his parents (Mary and Joseph) was complicated by claims that his biological father was the deity Jehovah. Some time after reaching adulthood, Jesus claimed to have had a mystical experience in which it was revealed to him that he was indeed the son of Jehovah, with a mission of saving humankind from the consequences of having sinned before the Lord. He traveled around that part of the world, preaching a message of love, forgiveness, and obedience to Jehovah. He also purported to have performed miracles to help the poor, sick, and outcast.*

When he refused to renounce the rumor that he was the son of God, he was denounced by some of the Jewish leaders, and then captured and crucified under orders of the Roman province governor, Pontius Pilate. He then claimed to have been revived from the dead, and to have joined Jehovah in Heaven.

Jesus claimed that his "second birth," this time as a full-grown man, began several days ago in Glacier County. He had no recollection of events prior to this. He spoke several languages fluently (including English), and claimed that his mission was to "save mankind from damnation."

MEDICAL HISTORY: *None reported, aside from scar tissue from deep wounds on the right side of his chest, the palms of both hands and the middle of both feet*

PSYCHIATRIC DIAGNOSES: *Paranoid schizophrenia, delusions of grandeur, post traumatic stress disorder from torture during imprisonment in his "first life," and a lack of any apparent support from family or friends*

*****

In our staff office, we gathered again to discuss how to handle this new case. The patient appeared to be less threatening than his predecessor, and might be more manageable in terms of treatment (particularly since he could speak English). We agreed that we needed to explore the background of his "second life" in some detail, and to understand how he came to be sitting near a camp for the homeless on a rainy night, and why he had refused a coat to protect himself against the rain. Was this part of a pattern of self-destruction, attention-seeking, or something else? In short, who was this man, and how could we help to bring him sanity and comfort in this challenging world?

CHAPTER THREE

Jesus C.

It was 5:15 p.m. when a tall, lanky social worker escorted a thin dark-skinned man with long hair and piercing black eyes into our office. The new patient was in his mid-thirties, and dressed in a black turtleneck shirt, dirty blue jeans, and sandals. He had a gold ring attached to his left ear, and a string of common stones around his neck. There was an air of confidence about him as he looked carefully at each one of us in the room, taking the measure of who we might be. When his gaze met mine, he smiled for no apparent reason.

I had been brought up in the western Episcopal tradition, with the belief that the real Jesus was white and looked like me and others in my community. This man's very dark skin color did not match my expectations. Then again, I had to remind myself that this was not the *real* Jesus. This was only a man who *believed* he was Jesus. The *real* Jesus had died two thousand years ago and had almost nothing to do with this impostor. I also knew that it was entirely possible that the real Jesus was likely to have been just as dark-skinned as the man before me.

There were the customary welcome pleasantries, during which Jesus nodded as each staff member was introduced. And then, since it was my job to do intake, I took Jesus aside to a small table in the dining room.

"Hi Jesus," I said. "My name is Patrick, and I'll be doing your admission to Rosewood."

As Jesus' dark eyes met mine, I noticed a surprising expression of warmth. "Patrick," he said, "I know all about you, and it is perfect that you should be the one to interview me here. We have much to talk about."

"What do you know about me?" I asked innocently.

He smiled and said, "I know that you, like me, have traveled to many places in the world, that you have an inquisitive mind, and a loving spirit that wants to help people."

I looked into his eyes for a while, speechless.

"I also know," he continued, "that your family lives seven miles east of Auburn on top of a ridge overlooking Lake Clementine. You are a musician, and your greatest desire is to stay alive for as many years as possible to give love and guidance to your seven-year-old daughter, Brigit."

I was not ready for this. It was much too personal, too perceptive, and too accurate for me to hear any more at this time. I needed to change the subject from me back to the man in front of me, whoever he was.

"Well, my friend," I said with a weak smile, "right now I need to learn about you. Let's begin with where you were born."

"Which life?" he replied in a matter-of-fact tone.

I recalled the two lives that had been listed on Jesus' discharge summary; the one 2,000 years ago, and the present one. I replied, "The most recent."

"You have read it in the hospital papers," he said. "This time I appeared here in Glacier County a few days ago. I know nothing more."

"Where is your family now?"

"I know nothing about the relatives of my present circumstance, and so far as I know, those from my past life are all quite dead. Fortunately, my present life, like my past life, is fully guided by my faith."

I didn't want to get into his faith just yet. That might be an endless journey leading just about anywhere. I continued, "How did you end up here in Roseville, California?"

"I don't know."

"Then please tell me what you were doing two nights ago, lying in the rain at the homeless camp and refusing to wear a coat?"

"I was praying."

"Were you aware of the dangers of exposure to the storm that night?"

"No. The storm didn't concern me."

"When the police put you in an ambulance and sent you to the Sutter-Roseville Hospital, how did you feel?"

"Good."

"Why?"

"Because I knew that I was on my way to Rosewood."

This answer was unexpected, and I didn't quite know how to respond. As I was puzzling over my next question, our other client, Adolph, walked into the dining room. He took one look at the dark-skinned man beside me, jumped on his back, and scratched his face terribly, while screaming unknown phrases in German.

I was slow to react this time, perhaps because I had been somewhat mesmerized by the man who was now a bloody mess. Eventually, two other social workers and I dragged Adolph off of Jesus, and led Adolph, still screaming epithets in German, back to the Quiet Room.

Nicholas, the Director of Rosewood, appeared, was apprised of what had just happened, and said that Adolph needed to be 5150ed as a danger to others in order to protect others from his fury.

The scene that followed was truly remarkable, for it unfolded in a strange swirl of fantasy and reality blended as one.

It started as two members of the Roseville Police Department put Adolph in handcuffs and on a gurney, and began dragging him away, kicking and screaming, through the Common Room and toward Rosewood's front door. Adolph yelled one more angry epithet in German toward Jesus, whose face was covered with blood, as it might have been when his namesake wore the crown of thorns.

Meanwhile, Jesus appeared to feel Adolph's pain. His face had an anguished look. Tears were streaming from both eyes, his knees were on the floor, and his hands were in a begging posture. He pleaded to Nicholas for Adolph to be allowed to stay at Rosewood. "I will take care of him!" came his now-booming voice. "I will nurture him and see that he harms no one! I will do this as God is my father. Trust me! Please trust me! Let Adolph stay here!"

Nicholas, who, unlike many mental health managers, had a kind and intuitive side, looked down at Jesus, felt the power of compassion, and said, "All right, Jesus. I'll take a chance this time. Adolph may stay. Officers, you may release the patient to our custody."

Before the police had a chance to respond, one of the upper-level managers of Glacier County Mental Health appeared on the scene. It was Program Manager Carrie Condor, a heavyset white woman with long auburn hair and eyes which, in situations like this, could spit fire like a dragon.

"What's going on here?" she shouted to one of the officers.

"We were preparing to take this patient to the Sutter-Roseville Hospital on a danger to others 5150."

"So what's the problem?"

"We were just told to release the patient to the custody of Rosewood."

"Is that true?" Carrie said to our poor Nicholas.

"Yes," he replied meekly.

"Well, I want this man put in handcuffs and taken to jail!" Carrie shouted for all to hear. "He's a danger to everyone and doesn't belong here!"

"Ma'am," said Jesus, now on the floor in a kneeling, supplicant posture, "I beg you, please let Adolph stay here. I will take responsibility." There was deep love in his voice, as he appealed to the compassionate side of Ms. Condor's nature. There was also a kind of calm resolution. My mind went back to the time when I heard Dr. Martin Luther King speak about the Mississippi Freedom Project at Stanford's Memorial Auditorium in March of 1964. No, the figure on his knees before me was no ordinary man.

Carrie's eyes looked down at this stranger, and said in a stern, condescending tone, "Young man, you have nothing to say about any of this!" Her message was clear: *Don't mess with me! I'm the one in control, and you are a nothing! I couldn't care less what you have to say, because I have power and you don't!* It felt to me like sheer ego—the kind that I had experienced so many times in my relations with Glacier County upper management. And now it was fascinating to watch these two forces clash—the evil one in my everyday work life, and this new inspiring one which had dropped mysteriously from the sky into our mental health world.

At this point, Jesus' eyes locked into those of Carrie in a kind of combat generally reserved for wrestlers on the mat or soldiers on the battlefield. Carrie tried to speak to give final orders for Adolph's removal, but the muscles around her mouth and tongue froze. She tried writing the orders with her right hand, but this limb also froze. Nicholas became concerned about what looked like Carrie having a stroke, and he ordered the waiting ambulance to take Carrie Condor (instead of Adolph) to the Sutter Roseville Hospital. Then, after Carrie was taken away, he ordered the officers to release Adolph, who ran back to his room. Jesus walked out to the patio, where he sat on the grass and went into some kind of trance. The rest of us returned to our office to ponder the miracle we had just witnessed.

There were several events subsequent to this incident which should be reported here. After an hour of treatment at the hospital, the muscle movement in Program Manager Carrie Condor's mouth, tongue and hand returned to normal, and she was released to her home. She made no further attempts to have Adolph sent to prison. The scars from the scratches on Jesus' face disappeared within the hour. When the night shift doctor was called in, he found that there was no evidence of cuts or bruises of any kind.

Finally, the two workers on the "noc" (graveyard) shift made a curious report. At 3:00 a.m., on their hourly resident bed check, they found Jesus missing from his room, and discovered him not only in Adolph's room, but in bed with Adolph, his arms wrapped around Adolph in a "spoons" position. Both residents appeared to be sleeping soundly, and the staff decided not to take action in this strange case (although such patient behavior was strictly prohibited), and to allow these two residents to continue sleeping as they were. One of the workers stated that he felt as though Jesus were "pouring a kind of spiritual energy into a fellow patient who was otherwise in great emotional pain."

*****

The next morning, at 7:45 a.m., we received a phone call notifying us of another incoming patient; and a short time later, there was a fax with this description:

PATIENT: *Joan Arc (alias Joan of Arc, Jehanne d'Arc, "the Maid of Orleans")*

RECENT HISTORY: *Patient is a white female, approximately 20 years old. She has been living for several weeks at the Good Hope battered women's shelter in Lincoln, California, where she spoke French and German. Two days ago she became highly manic and delusional, screaming to God to reveal His purpose for her in this life. When police arrived, she became catatonic and was 5150ed as gravely disabled to the Sutter Roseville Medical Center. After being medically cleared, she was sent to the Rosewood Psychiatric Facility.*

BACKGROUND: *Patient claims that she was born in 1412 A.D. in the French town of Domremy. She reported a Catholic upbringing during a period in which there were two contenders to the French throne, who eventually went to war to settle their differences. At the age of 12, she says that she had her first visions of Saint Michael, Saint Catherine, and Saint Margaret, who all told her to help drive out the pretender to the throne (the Duke of Burgundy) and to help place Charles VII in his rightful position. She reported that for the next several years she was active in helping to lead the armies of Charles VII in battle, which eventually led to Charles VII's coronation. She says she was later captured by the enemy at Campiegne, beaten and raped while in prison, and burned to death while tied to a pillar in Rouen in 1431. She claims that she has no idea how she happened to appear as a 20-year-old in 2008 in Lincoln, California, and wonders if her present life is a strange dream.*

MEDICAL HISTORY: *Evidence of beatings, rapes and severe burns on many parts of her body*

21

PSYCHIATRIC DIAGNOSES: *Schizophrenia, paranoid type, with auditory delusions relating to God; post traumatic stress syndrome from having been beaten, raped and severely burned; and no support from family or friends*

As the staff gathered around in our office to discuss this new patient, there was a serious tone. As with Jesus, we had rarely, if ever, experienced a person who had suffered so much in her short life. Regardless of the historical references, we couldn't begin to imagine what it would feel like if any of us had been subjected to such torture, and we became determined to treat both these new patients with great delicateness and compassion.

CHAPTER FOUR

Joan A.

At 9:15 a.m., an elderly veteran female social worker brought in an attractive, petite girl with very white skin, blue eyes, long blond hair, and an intense, haunted expression on her scarred face. The new patient was dressed in a dirty old white robe and sandals, and made little eye contact with any of our staff. The parts of her body which we could see—face, neck, and hands—had bruises and burns all over them, and we could only begin to guess what injuries might be present on the rest of her.

Since the patient spoke only French and German, and since I was the only staff member who spoke some French, I was called upon to translate. We went through the traditional welcome pleasantries, with the patient understanding my French much better than I could understand hers. Since the immediate setting did not lend itself to complexity, I think she got the message that this was to be her new home for a while, and that we would try to make her as comfortable as possible. During the intake, her answers followed the exact pattern as the history given in the discharge summary. She claimed to have been born and lived in what we would call medieval times, and to have followed the life of her famous namesake. She was very confused as to what she was doing alive in our time period, and she claimed that since she had already fulfilled her mission on Earth, she should be allowed to "stay dead in peace."

There was one curious item which Joan had brought with her—a large, very old, wooden trunk with faded paintings on top and a heavy lock. It took several minutes to open it, and inside was a complete suit of armor just her size, and a small, bejeweled sword. She smiled proudly as she picked up the sword to show it to me. "*Celui ci,*" she told me, "*c'est mon offertoire pour le bon Dieu.*" (This is my offering to the Lord.)

We took the trunk with the sword and armor to a special locked storage room, and left Joan in her new room for the next few hours. She was given a new blouse and pants to wear while her white robe was being washed and dried, and she welcomed the warm water in the shower in her room. She appreciated the large comb we gave her to straighten her hair, but didn't know what to do with the toothbrush and toothpaste. When I offered her fresh bread and milk, she devoured them with a nice smile.

It was just after noon when Joan walked down the hall to the dining room, where Jesus was sitting alone. Her first glance at him indicated mild interest. Then she sat down to eat a roast beef sandwich, and looked at him with a steady gaze.

At that moment, Jesus himself was engaged in a *sotto voce* prayer to offer gratitude to all the plants and animals who had given their lives that we might eat their bodies for this lunch. He was blessing them with a commitment to fuse their energies with his own, and thus give new vitality to our planetary community. When he was finished, I took the lead in introducing the new resident.

"Jesus," I said in French, "*je voudrais presenter notre residente nouvelle, Jehanne, qui va nous joindre pour un peu de temps.*" (This is our new resident, Joan, who will be joining us here for a while.)

As soon as I pronounced the word "Jesus," Joan's face turned ashen. She fell to her knees and put her hands together in the prayer position. "Jesus!" she called, and then again, and again, over and over. *Of course*, I thought. *She thinks this is the real Jesus, and that this is a vision from heaven.*

Jesus stood up and put his hand on her forehead. "My child," he said in French, "you are safe here, from all the troubles which you have suffered in your young life."

Nothing more was said for several minutes. She sobbed, and he embraced her and put his head against hers in a loving posture. I could only try to imagine what was going on in their minds.

Eventually Jesus suggested that she eat her food, and drink plenty of water—and that there would be lots of time later for the two of them to be together.

But no, this young girl was impatient, and she said to him, "Master, I need direction from you *now*! Please tell me this moment what I must do to serve the Lord! I have my sword and my armor. I have my frail body. And you have my total commitment to lead whatever armies you choose into battle to slay our enemies!"

Jesus met these words with a state of calm. He paused for a few seconds, carefully choosing his words. "Joan," he said, "I have no need of your sword, or of your armor."

"But Master," she replied, "many times have I proved myself on the battlefield, even killing grown men when given the opportunity."

"Joan, killing has never been my message." His voice was soft and sure.

"But Master, the three visions—of St. Michael, St. Catherine, and St. Margaret..."

"These were not visions of my Lord."

"Then how about my canonization by Pope Pius X? Am I not one of the most popular saints of the Catholic Church?"

Jesus looked at her again, and then looked down, slowly shaking his head sideways. In a measured tone, he said, almost mumbling, "Joan, my child, so much has been misinterpreted from my life and teachings. I hardly know where to begin."

Joan was distraught. "But you *do* recognize the Popes and the Catholic Church as your representatives on Earth."

"Oh, my child..." He didn't look up.

"What are you saying? Do you deny the existence of God through all that we know as holy in the world today?" She was screaming now, at the figure who, moments ago, she had revered. Jesus remained calm and quiet.

Joan's voice rose to a fever pitch as she yelled, "Impostor! Impostor! You are no Jesus! You are no son of God! You're a fraud, a traitor, an infidel!"

Had Joan possessed her sword at that moment, I have no doubt that she would have used it to try to sever Jesus' head from his body. As it was, two social workers and I put her in a restrained position, and led her, kicking and screaming, to the Quiet Room. Once there, she invoked the image of being burned again at the stake, and instructed us to kill her in the

26

most tortuous fashion possible in order to further beatify her soul before the *true* Jesus and the *true* Lord, who were waiting for her, once again, in Heaven. Her fury ended only after she was given a mild dose of morpheline, which slowed her energies and eventually put her to sleep.

Immediately after this incident, I felt a strong desire to speak to Jesus about what had just happened. However, this was not to be, for he withdrew immediately to a far corner of the patio, where he sat on a post and began praying to some remote, invisible figure in the sky.

*****

At 11:15 the next morning, we received a phone call from a local hospital informing us that another new resident would be coming to our facility. The fax on this new client came one hour later:

PATIENT: *Thomas Jefferson*

RECENT HISTORY: *Patient is a white male, 6'2" tall, 185 lbs., and approximately 80 years of age. Two days ago he had been seated on a chair in one of the courtrooms of the Placer County Courthouse in Auburn, when he suddenly arose to state an objection to a point blaming a man for refusing to pay his taxes. When asked by the judge to sit down and be quiet, he refused, stating that such taxes were inherently unfair and that a revolution was needed to overthrow the United States government.*

After being arrested on a charge of disorderly conduct, the patient was taken to Sutter Roseville Hospital, where it was discovered that he had no home and that he believed that he was the real Thomas Jefferson of early American History. He was 5150ed as gravely disabled and sent to the Rosewood Psychiatric Facility for treatment.

BACKGROUND: *Patient claimed he was born on April 13,*

1743, in a farmhouse in Northern Virginia. He says that although his parents were wealthy, with many slaves, he always felt uncomfortable about slavery. He reported loving the study of many subjects, from Latin to horticulture, but that his life was torn by the ravages of a revolutionary war and the tensions of disparate ideas in the building of a new nation. He says that the early death of his wife Martha was devastating, as was the publicity surrounding his relationship with his slave girl, Sally Hemings. Throughout his rise to the positions of Governor, Secretary of State, Vice President, and then President, he claimed that he maintained a cynical attitude toward the rulers of all political systems, and thus took little pleasure in watching the shaky development of the country he had helped to found. Migraine headaches and poor eyesight (reducing his ability to read) had contributed to major depression in the later stages of this life.

Just prior to his death at his home in Monticello, patient reports praying to God "for an opportunity to continue a form of life in which I could witness future events in my nation and my planet." Then, after his death in 1826, he claimed that he lived a strange "spirit-life" in which his mind was able to follow such major developments. He claimed that he experienced the horrors of the Civil War during the presidency of Abraham Lincoln, the brutalizing of both Indians and Negroes during the Reconstruction Period, the excesses of capitalism during the period of the Robber Barons, and the craziness of the wars with Mexico in 1846, Spain in 1898, and Europe during 1914-1918. He saw America develop into a bully nation in its relation to its Latin American neighbors, and later toward Vietnam and Iraq. He also witnessed the Great Depression of the 1930s, and World War II in its aftermath. He claimed to have been fascinated with the development of theories by such men as Charles Darwin, Karl Marx, Sigmund Freud, Albert Einstein, John Maynard Keynes, and Milton Friedman. He claimed to have been very excited by the civil rights movements led by people like Elizabeth Cady Stanton, Jane Addams, Rev. Martin Luther King Jr., Cesar Chavez, Gloria Steinem and others. He felt eternally grateful to have been able to follow developments in such diverse fields as architecture, medicine, and politics, even though his was but the role of an observer.

Patient went on to state that "with all this in my mind, I was stunned to find myself suddenly thrust, several days ago, into the body of an octogenarian watching a trial in Auburn, California." He further stated, "In my eternal quest to discover more about the nature of God, the universe, and myself, I am finding that the only constant is the element of surprise."

MEDICAL HISTORY: *Frequent migraine headaches; compound fracture of his left wrist, untreated and allowed to become deformed; major back pain; rheumatism*

PSYCHIATRIC DIAGNOSES: *Major depressive disorder, recurrent, moderate, schizoaffective disorder, with delusions of grandeur*

As the staff gathered in the office to discuss this new patient, I became silent in a kind of reverie, for this particular historical figure, along with Jesus, were perhaps my greatest heroes. Real or not, I felt inadequate to the task of treatment.

*****

At this time, I feel a need to add something that is totally inappropriate. While interviewing Joan of Arc in the dining room, my eyes suddenly became fixated on the sight bulge of Joan's small breasts, which were pushing softly against her white robe. I don't know why. Maybe it had something to do with France, or her unmitigated passion, or even the thought of her sweet, innocent skin, being torched at the stake. Yes, I was quite aware of the Rosewood rules, and that any conduct in this direction would be a really stupid way of getting fired. I just mention it here, in passing.

CHAPTER FIVE

Tom J.

Have you ever felt really excited about going to work? That's how I began to feel during this period, as each day passed and each new patient arrived at Rosewood. I couldn't wait to walk through that front door and hear what our patients had done overnight, and who might be coming to our crisis facility this next day. The noc staff reported that all three of our current residents (Adolph, Jesus and Joan) were able to communicate in German, a language which none of us knew. And of course, we could expect that our next patient, the super-educated Thomas Jefferson, would also speak fluent German. So there we were, a staff limited for the most part to English, with a clientele for whom German was the common language.

The isolation which Adolph had manifested in his first few days changed markedly after the incident in which Jesus had successfully pleaded for his continued stay at Rosewood. The two of them held long conversations in the patio, in which Adolph emoted with expressions of great excitement, loud laughter, and deep sobbing. On several occasions I can remember thinking *I wish to Hell I knew what they were talking about!* The frustration grew as I pondered the reality that Jesus had become Adolph's real confidant and social worker, not me! When, on one occasion, I asked Jesus what kind of things Adolph was saying, he replied that this was between the two of them, and that he did not want to violate that confidence.

Joan, on the other hand, remained distant from Jesus. Since that inflamed episode when she denounced him as an imposter, she had avoided him. There were no more such outbreaks, but she was clearly not about to renew even cordial relations. Strangely, she grew closer to Adolph, who in our world was older than Jesus and had become a kind of father figure. For Adolph's part, he appeared to see in her a non-threatening innocence, and perhaps a kind of fertility hope for the white race. He also enjoyed her militance.

Meanwhile, Jesus himself became an increasing enigma. He was most comfortable when trying to solve the problems of others, and became reticent when asked to discuss his own life

32

and problems. The symptoms of his mental illness were difficult to pin down. Surely he was delusional about being the original Christ and the son of God, but this belief rarely came up in conversations. I sensed that there were some deep-seeded feelings of guilt and anger, which needed time to come out into the open.

*****

At 2:30 p.m., a young social female worker escorted an elderly new patient into our office, He was 6' 2" tall, slender, and somewhat slow in his movements. He was white-skinned, with thinning hair and a shy manner. He was dressed in a ruffled rose-colored shirt, light blue pants, and black slipper-shoes, all from the early 19th century. He, too, brought with him a large trunk. But unlike Joan's trunk, this one was filled with old books, papers and scientific instruments.

"Good afternoon, citizens," he said in a soft tone as he walked through the door. "Is this to be my new home?"

The highest-ranking person on duty at that time was a man called Craig, who had a mellow voice and a background in American Literature. "Good sir," he said, "it is indeed an honor to welcome the sage of Monticello to our premises. Our abode is humble compared to yours, but we are truly your most obedient servants, who will endeavor to assist you in every way."

Thomas Jefferson smiled at him and replied, "The honor is all mine. And your eloquence belies your common attire. But please tell me now, what is the time and place of my presence at this moment? You see, I am more than a little confused as to my circumstances."

"The year is 2012," Craig replied, "and the place is Rosewood, a mental health facility in Roseville, California." He thought for a moment, and added, "in the United States of America."

As Craig spoke, my thoughts went back to the real Monticello in Northern Virginia, which I had visited several times. I suddenly wanted to take our new guest there, and show him how almost nothing had changed. The large pillars at the portal and the Italian-style dome were all polished to a bright white. The grand clock made of weights was still over the front door, and the busts of Rousseau, Voltaire, and other heroes of Jefferson in the hallway were all dusted and aligned. Most of the original paintings by masters had been preserved and maintained in their proper places on the walls, and Jefferson's own bed, purposefully placed between the salon and his study, was ready for him to crawl into.

"Has anyone else from my time period come to your world?" he asked, breaking my reverie. "Most particularly my wife Martha, my slave girl Sally Hemings, President Washington, Colonel Lafayette, or the venerable John Adams?"

"No," Craig replied. He added, "Not to our knowledge."

Thomas Jefferson looked directly at the board on which were written the first names of the other current residents. "Hmm," he said in a drawn-out manner. "Adolph...Hitler, Jesus...Christ. Joan...of Arc. And me...I must be in some kind of purgatory. This is all too unreal."

There was silence throughout the small office as we all thought the same thing. Yes, this was unreal. Having one such celebrity might not be noteworthy. Having two could be an interesting coincidence. But four patients with famous names in one facility, each of whom truly believed that he or she was their historical namesake! This was far beyond random probability. Either it was some large-scale joke, a contrived sociological experiment, or some other mystery waiting to be solved.

"Well, kind sirs," said our new guest, "I find this all to be fascinating, and I shall look forward to your explanations of our common reality. By the way," he continued, "do you have a library?"

"Our library," Craig responded, "could never begin to match yours at Monticello." (Ours consisted of a few Stephen King and Danielle Steele novels, a *Bible*, and a couple of books from Alcoholics Anonymous.) "However," Craig continued, "we could try to procure any books you desire. We also have internet access, and a new book invention called Kindle."

Our guest's eyes lit up, and he said, "Yes, yes, I have heard reference to such things, but have not yet had an opportunity to observe them."

At this point, an eager Thomas Jefferson was given the tour of our modest premises, read the rules, and shown where to sign the necessary papers to make him an official resident. Laundry was a concern of his, and he was shown our washer and dryer (which amazed him) and told that he would need to push the proper buttons and fold the clean clothes himself, which he agreed to do in spite of a remark that this kind of work should be done by slaves. He was given a change of clothes—a yellow and blue tee shirt reading "UCLA," and some blue jeans and sneakers, which he put on with a hearty laugh.

*****

One hour later, I knocked on Tom's door and told him that we needed more information about his life and mental health. He suggested that we go for a ride, and asked whether there were two good horses at the facility. I told him that this would not be possible, since times had changed and horses were rarely used in today's world.

"What a pity," he answered. "Through the years, this noble beast has softened the harshness of life in a thousand ways."

I arranged for us to drive to one of the local parks in a county car. He was fascinated by our county's white Taurus, and insisted on looking under the hood. He even squeezed under the car to check out the way the wheels moved. Later, he remarked at how close together the houses were, and at the scarcity of trees, meadows and farmland. "Mankind," he said, "appears to be abusing Mother Nature, and nothing good can come of this."

When we arrived at Maidu Park, we took a trail along a creek and I began asking him about his recent life. "What can you tell me about how you came to be in the Auburn Courthouse yesterday?"

"Nothing," he replied. "I have no explanation."

"Then please tell me why you objected so strongly when the judge ordered the man to pay his back taxes."

"Having listened to all the arguments, I felt that this man should not be forced to support an inept government and a senseless war."

"How did you feel when you were arrested?"

"I felt fine." The next words were delivered in a surprisingly angry tone. "Patrick, I sense that for some reason you are choosing to ignore the larger picture."

"What larger picture?"

"The fact is that my name is Thomas Jefferson, and that I had a full life some two hundred years ago. I wrote the first draft of the Declaration of Independence, and more than 20,000 letters. You may test me on all of this, and while you're at it, test my blood, my bones, the clothes I was wearing when arrested, and the books in that trunk. Something very strange is happening, and it has nothing to do with mental health."

I was quiet for a while. The last thing I wanted to do was alienate the namesake of the man whom I admired perhaps more than anyone in history! But I also needed to write my report about this patient's current mental condition, and to put something down on his 21st century life.

"Thomas," I said, "protocol requires me to ask you about how you feel now—whether you are depressed, and whether you hear voices or are having hallucinations. And after we discuss these things, then we can move on to what you call the larger picture."

"How do I feel now?" he mimicked. "I feel many emotions. I'm elated to have a body once more, and to be walking in the fresh air! I'm in awe of the technology I see around me! I'm thrilled to be able to read once again. And I'm frustrated to be contained in this mental health world of yours! I love to write letters, but I'm tormented in having no one to write to! I want to have friends, and to talk with them about everything from philosophy to flowers. I notice that Jesus' name is on your board. I haven't met him yet, but whoever he is, I want to go somewhere with him and ask him a thousand questions! And yes, I still have migraine headaches, but I don't see a need to dwell on them—there's much more to life than a few aches and pains. Does that begin to answer your questions?"

"Yes," I said. "Thank you."

"And there's more," he continued in an angry tone. "You can call these delusions, but I miss my wife, my children, my grandchildren, my slaves, and my many friends. Yes, I also miss Maria (presumably Cosway, his European paramour). I will never forgive Aaron (Burr) for killing Alex (Hamilton), and I will never forgive Tom (Callendar) for spreading lies about Sallie (Hemings). Yes, I may be a ghost from the past, but I am alive and real and full of the entire range of emotions which make us human. And you can take your God-Damned mental health questions and go to Hell!"

*****

One hour later another phone call came in from an outlying hospital, and this fax appeared:

PATIENT: *Ludwig Van Beethoven*

RECENT HISTORY: *Patient is a 5' 6" husky, elderly man, who was found trying to break into the St. Joseph's Cathedral in Rocklin, California. The Rocklin Police reported (through a sign language interpreter) that he said he wanted to play the large organ there, and nothing more. When asked his identity, he reported in written form that he was Ludwig Van Beethoven, the famous composer who has been dead for two hundred years, and that he had no living friends or family. He said he had no idea how he had arrived in Rocklin, California. He was taken to the Sutter Psychiatric Facility for an assessment.*

BACKGROUND: *Patient claimed that he had been born in*

1770 in Brabant, Belgium, where his alcoholic father was a musician at the Court of Bonn. At the age of seven, he said he gave his first concert in Cologne. At the age of 17, he claims to have gone to Vienna, where he was tutored by Mozart, and then Haydn. His many compositions began with piano sonatas, and expanded into full orchestral symphonies and one opera—Fidelio. In 1801, he began to lose his hearing, which made him "furious at the unfairness of life." Nevertheless, the patient claimed that he continued to compose, even while deaf. He struggled to overcome financial challenges, while keeping such company as Franz List, Gioachino Rossini and Franz Schubert, and he came to be recognized as the greatest composer of his day. Patient claims to have died during a storm in March of 1827, and has no idea how he was revived in the twenty-first century.

In today's world, patient claimed to have "no friends, no family, no home, and no desire in life except to compose and play music."

MEDICAL HISTORY: *Deafness, since the age of 35, and related anger and depression*

PSYCHIATRIC DIAGNOSES: *Schizoaffective, with delusions of grandeur; severe depression with anxiety, and intermittent explosive disorder*

"Fascinating" was the word most used most by the staff as we contemplated this next arrival of a celebrity from history.

*****

Meanwhile, at home, my daughter Brigit expressed an interest in the only female resident at Rosewood. When I described Joan as a young French woman who believed that she had led armies in a former life, Brigit asked, "Is she pretty?"

"Yes."

"Is she married?"

38

"No."

"Do you like her?"

"She's nice."

"Does she like you?"

"I have no idea."

Of course, Brigit's interest in this was to have some kind of mother. I was not about to even think of anything like this. Despite my recent libidinous thoughts, the notion of having a romantic relationship with someone thirty years younger (or thirteen hundred years older), and who actually believed that she was Joan of Arc, was totally absurd.

CHAPTER SIX

Ludwig B.

"I'm so sorry!" Tom exclaimed when I arrived at Rosewood the next morning. "My behavior yesterday was inexcusable, and I must try to make it up to you."

"Don't worry about it, Tom," I replied. "I'm sure you had a hundred things on your mind. Besides, I was insensitive and shouldn't have pushed the mental health questions on you so fast."

"Just for the record," Tom continued, "from an early age, I have grown accustomed to being treated with the respect owed to the aristocracy, and later on, to one of the founders and leaders of our country. Everyone from General George Washington to King Louis XVI and King George III has viewed me as a figure of importance, with a brilliant mind and transformational ideas. The fixation here on mental health is understandable in the circumstances, but difficult for me to tolerate. I want to talk about the state of our country and our world, not about the severity or lack thereof of my personal depression. And I would truly like to meet with the scholars, scientists, and political leaders of your day, instead of trying to help you diagnose what you consider to be a grand delusion."

*****

At 9:30 a.m., one social worker, a German translator, and two members of the Roseville Police Department, escorted a man of about fifty-five, with long white hair, pock marks on his reddish facial skin, and a bearing of contempt for everyone around him, through the front door of Rosewood. He stood 5' 7", weighed about 180 lbs., was dressed in a dark coat and pants dating from the mid-19th century, and was hunched over in a posture that indicated a life of mental and physical challenges.

"Ludwig," the social worker told us, "is totally deaf. He cannot read lips, cannot understand English, and has no knowledge of our modern sign language. All our communication with him will have to be in writing through interpreters."

Nicholas, our Rosewood leader, asked the interpreter to

write on a pad of paper, "Welcome, Ludwig! We hope to make you happy in our Rosewood home."

The man looked at this note, and gave us all a sneer of disgust. Then he wrote on the same pad of paper, a note which was translated as follows: "This is not the kind of home to which I have grown accustomed. Further, I have no need of any of your services, except for a pad like this one for the composition of music."

"Very well," Nicholas told the German translator to write on the next page of the pad. "You may keep this pad, and we will give you as many more as you desire."

As we brought Ludwig across the office portal and into the Rosewood Common Room, we found that all our patients were gathered there. Adolph was pacing back and forth in a space near the hallway. Jesus was engaged in a conversation with Tom, and Joan was seated by herself in a corner with a strained expression on her face.

"Members of Rosewood," I said to the group, "it is my pleasure to introduce to you a new member of our community, Ludwig Van Beethoven." Jefferson translated this to German for those who didn't speak English.

As soon as this had been translated, Adolph yelled out something in German which was later translated to me as, "You God-Damned bastards! Here you go again, pretending to bring in people from history to make me think that I'm crazy! Well I'm on to your game! This man is no more the great composer than Jesus or Jefferson are the people they are portraying! They are all just actors, and I'm not going to take any more of this bullshit!"

To this, Ludwig, whom we all thought was deaf, screamed back at Adolph in perfect German, a statement that was later translated to me as, "I don't know who you are, but you can go straight to hell! I happen to be the finest musician our civilization has ever produced, and if you don't apologize at once, I shall see you dead within the minute!"

As the Rosewood staff, myself included, leaned forward to

restrain the adversaries, there was more shouting. Adolph challenged Ludwig to "play a single note" on the piano; and Ludwig accepted the challenge, while calling Adolph various profanities in German. There was a move to guide both of these patients to the Quiet Room, but once again Jesus intervened.

"Ladies and gentlemen," he said calmly, "I propose that we settle this matter here and now by creating the conditions for a simple recital. If we can make arrangements to have both of these men released to my custody, then I will accept responsibility for channeling their energies into a performance of benefit to everyone."

Once again, Nicholas agreed to follow the suggestion of Jesus. Both adversaries were released and sat across the room from each other in cold silence. Jesus proceeded to motion everyone—staff and patients alike—to one side of the room, and to create, with a wave of his hands, an antique grand piano and stool.

Suddenly, into this already surrealistic scene, the figure of Lucy Loon, Assistant Director of Glacier County's mental health system, appeared in the Common Room.

"Has no one read the county rules?" she exclaimed. "Pianos are strictly prohibited in this building, and I should like this one to be removed immediately!" She looked at Nicholas, who gave this simple reply: "Yes, Ms. Loon, right away. Of course, it will be difficult to remove, since it is larger than any of the doors leading out of this room."

"I don't care how large it is!" Ms. Loon bellowed. "I want it out of here, *now*!" She looked at a fire extinguisher and axe on the wall and shouted, "Use this God-Damned fire ax if you need to, and break it into little pieces!"

"Ma'am," said the generally soft-spoken Jesus in a tone of voice that indicated that his patience with county management was once again wearing thin, "I would request that before you do this, we allow our new patient here to play something on this finely fashioned instrument."

"Young man," she replied, echoing the words and tone of

voice used by Program Manager Cassie Condor not long ago. "Let me remind you who is in charge here. It is *me*—not you! And I have given the order for the immediate destruction of this piano!"

Adolph, seeing the intransigence of Ms. Loon, and recalling what had happened to Ms. Condor in a similar circumstance not long ago, began to laugh hysterically. I must confess that I too was holding back a grin.

And so it was that the face of Ms. Loon began to turn purple; and in short order, her body began to rise helplessly off of the Rosewood Common Room floor. Her face then turned green, and it assumed various contorted expressions as her voice emitted confused noises,

"Jesus!" Nicholas exclaimed in a clear, firm voice, "would you please arrange for Ms. Loon to be restored to her normal condition? I'm sure she's sorry for what she said, and we don't need any more people going to the hospital."

Jesus, whose gaze had been fixed on Ms. Loon during this time, waved his hand and made her disappear. "She's back in her office," he said. "Her body is fine, and I don't think she'll be bothering us again today."

With this taken care of, a furious Ludwig gave Adolph a murderous look before striding over to the piano, sitting on the bench in front of it, and playing the *Moonlight Sonata*. The touch of his fingers on the keys was extraordinary as he moved through the haunting beauty of this piece, and into an abbreviated version of Richard Wagner's opera *Tristan Und Isolde*, which was delivered with a brief wink at Adolph. His closing piece was an excerpt from the *maitre d'oeuvre* of his career, *Ode to Joy*. Each note was perfect in its strength and timing. Each chord had just the right feeling, and each movement of his hands was synchronized with a matching emotion emanating from his eyes.

It was the performance of a lifetime for each of us. When it was over, we sat in silence, moved beyond words and applause, indeed, not wanting this joyous time to ever end. Even Adolph had, on his usually severe face, the smile of a happy child.

*****

Later that day, Tom called me aside and made an unusual request. "Patrick," he said, "I have a favor to ask you. Ever since I arrived here at Rosewood, I have been wanting to have a personal conversation with Jesus. But every time I try, we seem to be interrupted by others who also want to talk with him. Could you possibly arrange for the three of us to meet somewhere outside of Rosewood, where I could ask him some questions and hear his answers, with no distractions?"

"Yes, of course," I said, knowing that I was just as interested as Tom in such a meeting.

CHAPTER SEVEN

the River

Ten miles east of our Rosewood facility, there is a beautiful spot where the North and Middle Forks of the American River come together. I received special permission to drive Jesus and Jefferson to this confluence on a crisp sunny day in November. For Rosewood purposes, the mission was part of their therapy. For Jefferson and me, the mission was to satisfy an immense curiosity. For Jesus, I suspect it was tolerated as part of a credo of not refusing a reasonable request from one of his brethren.

The oak leaves were turning brown, and the sun was sparkling on the ripples of water as they flowed over the mossy rocks. Families of quail stepped sprightly along the trail in front of us, while a red-tailed hawk circled overhead. It was a magnificent day! Had I been a filmmaker, I would have worked hard to capture this remarkable event for posterity. As it was, the only record kept of this singular occurrence is in the form of the paltry lines of this book. Nevertheless, I shall do my best to describe the scene to you.

As soon as we arrived at a set of rocks where we could sit and watch the water, Jefferson said to Jesus, "Good Sir, I am truly honored and appreciative that you agreed to spend these few hours here with me."

"Don't mention it," Jesus replied in a soft but distant tone.

"I have just a few questions for you," Jefferson continued. "Certainly there are many more in my mind, but I do not wish to overburden you, and a response to these few would do much to appease my hungry soul."

"You may proceed."

"My first question is one which I suspect led you into deep trouble with both the Pharisees and the Romans, and which may have been the immediate cause of your crucifixion."

"Yes?"

"Could you tell me whether or not you are the son of God?"

Jesus' gaze was fixed on a distant rock downstream. He did not reply.

"I have read," Jefferson continued, "that you were asked

on numerous occasions whether you were the biological son of God, and each time your answer was ambiguous. The four gospels all claim that you were born of the Virgin Mary, and conceived not by her husband Joseph, but by God Himself. Is this your belief too?"

Jesus' eyes remained fixed on the distant rock, and he did not reply for a long time. At last, he turned to Jefferson and gave this answer, "I will try," he said in a soft tone, "to answer each of your questions as best as I can. But before I begin, let me caution you that my own views should not be taken as what you might call Gospel Truth. No, they are the thoughts of a very human creature who, like you, is also struggling to understand the complexity of life, the universe, and our place in it."

He paused before offering this remarkable answer. "Of course, the details of my conception are totally unknown to me. And neither of my parents (Joseph and Mary) ever mentioned the possibility of an immaculate conception until I was fully grown. You should note here that at the time of my birth, there was a massive hunt for newborn male babies, and that many were killed for no reason other than the timing of their births. So if the Lord were my biological father, it would not be the kind of thing one would talk about, even with close friends. You should also bear in mind how such a topic might subject our family to ridicule, as well as danger. No, the truth is that I have no way of knowing my precise biology, any more than you do."

"Then," said Jefferson, "a related question would be about the relationship you have with the Lord. Does He treat you like a son in some way? Do you have a special way of conversing with him, or of asking him questions about your fears and doubts? Has he ever manifested himself to you in some form, physical or metaphysical?"

Jesus looked directly at Jefferson and replied, "My good man, the truth is that these questions are beyond my power to answer. Yes, I have a relationship with Him which is powerful beyond words. And yes, we communicate on very personal and profound levels. But then again, I believe that every single one of us is a child of the Lord, communicating with Him in unique ways."

"I guess my real question, " Jefferson continued, " is whether you feel that the Lord placed you on this planet to ultimately suffer on the cross and thus save mankind from damnation."

"My honest answer," Jesus replied, "is that I believe that my purpose here on Earth has been to try to steer humanity toward a more kind and gentle nature. Questions such as whether or not I am the biological son of God, whether or not my crucifixion served to save humankind from some kind of original sin, or whether or not I arose from the dead in some godly manner—all these have served primarily to distract humankind from the essence of my teaching, which is to love one another."

"Then," Jefferson continued, "that leads me to my next question. With all of your emphasis on love—on turning the other cheek, loving thine enemies, etc.—how do you feel about the many innocent people who have been killed in your name, in the Crusades, the Spanish Inquisition, the slaughter of Native Americans, and the various institutions of slavery, in which I, too, have been complicit. Even recent wars such as in Afghanistan, Iraq, and Vietnam have invoked your name in support of the killing of others. How do you feel about all this?"

Jesus turned to look down on the small rocks below him, and he wept. Tears fell uncontrollably, and he rubbed his eyes with both hands. In a motion I shall never forget, Jefferson walked over and put a comforting arm around Jesus' shoulder.

Jesus said, "Excuse me," and he walked behind a group of boulders and out of sight. He remained there for several minutes before returning to us. I speculated that this might have been anything from a time to pee to a time to pray.

At last, he began to answer Jefferson's question. "I have failed," Jesus told him openly. "I honestly don't know how I could have made my message more clear. And yet, as you say, the history is there. People, particularly rulers, but also common farmers, merchants, and others, have claimed to be my followers while engaging in the killing of others. This is the exact opposite of the message I sought to convey. Why did it happen? I don't know. Maybe something to do with mankind's ego, or an inherent need for power. I don't know. It all seems so perverted, so hypocritical, so crazy!"

"But Jesus," Tom replied, "so many of your followers have brought love and service in a million ways to humankind. Think of St. Francis of Assisi, Mother Teresa, and others. One could say that your love has been your greatest legacy."

After another silence, Jefferson said, "My next question is about the difference between the Old Testament and the New Testament, indeed between Judaism and Christianity. As you may be aware, during my life in Monticello, I kept what has come to be known as the *Jefferson Bible*. This contained excerpts of my favorite passages in the *New Testament*. Conspicuously absent is the god of wrath which is so dominant in the *Old Testament*, whereby sinners were cursed rather than forgiven, and innocent people were destroyed by floods and warfare. My question is how can you reconcile the teachings of the god of the *Old Testament* with those you brought to the world in the *New Testament*?"

Again Jesus was quiet for a long time before answering. At last he said, "Thomas, your perspective is exactly right. My ideas were revolutionary, and in some ways they still are. Had I been living at the time of Cain or Noah, I would have protested the treatment of their families and friends, and I probably would have been killed for this. But your question is also about whether or not my god is the same as the god of Genesis. And this I cannot answer. Those events took place long before I was born, and were written down by people whom I never knew. Like you in your *Jefferson Bible*, I chose to ignore those stories, because the messages in them so disagreed with my own beliefs."

After a pause, Jefferson said, "My next question also reaches back in time long before you were born, and I suspect that your answer will be similarly challenging. But I will ask the question anyway. What can you tell us about the creation?"

At this, Jesus' face broke into a large grin. "Thomas," he

said, "you certainly know how to challenge the mind. And you are quite right. I really have no more insight into the original creation than you."

"But," Jefferson continued, "let me trace my logic on this, even though you may not have an answer. Our very existence seems like a contradiction. How could the Creator create Himself? From what, and with what tools? In terms of this initial creation, the concepts of both existence and God make no sense at all."

Still smiling, Jesus said, "Perhaps your sense of logic is an inappropriate approach to such a question. In any case, your perceived conundrum is real, and my relationship with the Lord has given me no clue as to an answer."

"Here's another question that perhaps you cannot answer," said Jefferson, "because it relates more to the domain of God than to the domain of the son of God. But it has been burning in my mind for a long time, so I will ask it anyway. If God is truly the Creator of all that is in the universe, then He must have created evil. If so, He would be ultimately responsible for all the suffering of innocent babies, and of victims of the Nazi Holocaust, and for other horrid episodes in human history. How does He feel about this? Is the answer that cruelty and suffering are a necessary part of life—like the *yin* and *yang* of Buddhism? And that, strangely, the world needs cruelty every bit as much as it needs love and good deeds? Do we need people like our housemate Adolph every bit as much as we need people like yourself? Or maybe the answer is that, in the final analysis, there is no good or evil—everyone acts according to what they believe is called for at that moment in time. What do you think?"

"Your original premise is right," Jesus replied. "As the so-called son of God, I have no way of knowing how to answer these questions. For this, you would need the Lord Himself, and access to Him for these kinds of questions would be difficult."

"Then please tell me this," Jefferson persisted. "In your life long ago, how did you select those whom you helped by miracles, and select out those whom you didn't help?'

"To be honest, I never thought much about it. I simply helped those around me who appeared to be in need at the time."

"All right," said Jefferson, "then let me move on to another subject. How do you view such religious leaders as Abraham, Moses, Mohammed and Buddha? Do you see yourself as different and unique, or as part of a common energy united with them to lead mankind to a better place?"

"Ahh," said Jesus, "this is a question to which I can give you a more direct answer. To be perfectly honest, I find that my teachings have much more in common with those of Siddhartha (Buddha), than those of Abraham, Moses or Mohammed. Siddhartha and I both championed the practice of pacifism and forgiveness, while war and retribution have been a vital part of the beliefs of the others. Siddhartha and I are both committed to compassion for all, while the others believe in the concept of a chosen people and a kind of outcast state for non-believers. Although some of my own followers continue to kill in what might be misguidedly called 'holy wars,' and to discriminate against females, gays, lesbians, people of color, and many others, both Siddhartha and I are united in believing that all humans should be given full respect, and treated equally."

"Then tell me now how this factors into your view of Heaven and Hell? Haven't you maintained that those who do not follow the teachings of the Lord will go to Hell, the ultimate rejection, or the ultimate intolerance? Please tell me more about what these terms mean."

"Ahhh, my friend," said Jesus, smiling again. "It's been a long time since I had a conversation like this one. Can I let you in on a little secret?"

"Of course," said Jefferson with a smile, and I leaned closer to hear every word.

In a low whisper and a devilish grin, Jesus told us, "I invented the concepts of Heaven and Hell in order to give my teachings a little push. The truth is that at that time I had no way of knowing what would happen to any of us after death, and I was getting discouraged about the way people paid almost no attention to what I was saying. *Blessed are the meek, for they shall inherit the earth. Blessed are the peacemakers, for they shall be called the children of God...* Even back then, in my first life, I could tell that my message was not being comprehended, much less followed. It was too radical for that time, and I'm afraid that these ideas are still too radical for most people here in the twenty-first century."

Jefferson looked shocked. "Are you telling us that you lied back then? That you bore false witness?"

"I wouldn't exactly call it that. Note that I was never specific about just what Heaven and Hell meant. I never actually described them, and I never really said that they occurred after death. What I was thinking is that both states can occur during life to those who follow their conscience, or follow the other side. Heaven and Hell can occur during normal life for each one of us. They are states of mind and soul."

"Then let me move on to the crucifixion. That must have been excruciating, and must have made you question your whole relationship with God. How could He have both loved you and put you through such pain?"

"Yes, agony. It's hard for anyone to imagine what torment my body endured during those hours...days. Fortunately, I was unconscious much of the time. But when I was awake, I did wonder how could this be happening to me, and why."

"Many Christians interpret your crucifixion as the most important part of your life, for your suffering on the cross saved all mankind from our sins. What do you think of this?"

"It's an interesting theory. But to be truthful, while I was in agony on the cross, there was not a single thought like that. I was just totally crazy and confused. My body hurt so much that I don't think my mind was capable of working— much less of conceiving this kind of rationalization as to why I had been put through this, if indeed there was a reason. It wasn't until long after my death that others concluded that somehow my suffering and death could save mankind from original sin. I don't exactly know how this connection could be made. It seems like such a stretch. But it made a lot of people feel better about themselves and their faith. So I guess it became encoded in the thinking of many Christians.

"The thing that really burns me up," Jesus continued, in a tone of rising anger, "is that especially if future Christians believed that I had suffered on the cross for them, they *still* ignored my teachings! And the truth is that I don't know if I can ever forgive them for this! It's so horrible!"

There was another pause at this point, with Thomas Jefferson cradling Jesus in his arms, and both men crying. After taking a deep breath, Jesus went on.

"So many Christians, over the years, have lived lives of greed and selfishness, and have supported slavery and those terrible wars. Of the religious leaders you mentioned earlier, who was the only one whose followers actually lived lives of peace and humility? Certainly not mine! And not those of Moses, or Mohammed! No, it was the followers of Siddartha! And he didn't even have to die on a cross to get his message across!" The tone in Jesus' voice was rising, and again his anger was showing through.

Jefferson waited an appropriate time before asking his next question. "So Jesus," he said softly, "do you think that are there major differences between your teachings and those of Buddha?"

"I don't know," he answered. "Buddha appears to have guided people toward a somewhat vague form of enlightenment through a rejection of ego and an acceptance of life as it is. And I have guided mine toward the pursuit of love through a personal commitment to a real person called the Lord. There are great differences, as well as similarities."

After another silent period, Tom said, "Jesus, please tell me more about your thoughts on Mohammed."

More silence.

"Thomas, again I will be very honest with you. Just as I have had trouble with the concept of the chosen people of the Old Testament, I have had trouble with some of the intransigent qualities of Islam. Its insistence that Mohammed is the ultimate prophet for all mankind, that the *Qu'ran* is the only spiritual book and cannot be translated into other languages, and that such acts as stoning and polygamy are acceptable— all these bother me. Still, I believe that Mohammed's strong belief in mercy comes close to my belief in love. And he was, by and large, a peaceful man."

The sun was falling low in a pink sky, and Jesus looked exhausted, so we decided to hike back up to the car and return to Rosewood. When Jefferson mentioned that he would like to have this kind of discussion again, Jesus lowered his eyebrows and muttered, "We'll see."

*****

After walking through the modest front door at Rosewood, I noticed another name on our patient board: "Sid G." *At last,* I thought, *we'll have someone normal, as opposed to a celebrity from times past.* But such was not to be. I looked at the faxed materials and read the following:

PATIENT: *Siddhartha Gautama (alias Buddha)*

RECENT BACKGROUND: *Patient is a 5'4" obese Asian man in his mid-60s. He was found sitting with a grin, crosslegged, underneath a large sequoia tree near the town of Foresthill. When police tried to communicate with him, he did not respond at all. Documents in his clothing indicated that his name was Siddhartha Gautama, and that some people referred to him as "The Buddha." He was 5150ed as gravely disabled and taken to Sutter Roseville Hospital. The next day he awakened from his trance and spoke in English about his life.*

HISTORY: *Patient claimed to have been born in Lumbini, in what is now known as Nepal, around 563 B.C. He claimed to have been the son of a king, and to have renounced his royal status in favor of a mission to eliminate suffering from the world. He discovered "Four Noble Truths," and then spent the rest of his life urging people to let go of all desires and attachments. He claims to have died around 483 B.C., and has no explanation for what happened between then and the moment he was found in Foresthill two days ago.*

MEDICAL DIAGNOSIS: *Obese, with related high cholesterol and blood pressure*

PSYCHIATRIC DIAGNOSIS: *Schizophrenia, with delusions of grandeur and hallucinations*

My thoughts raced to the unlikely event of someone who called himself Buddha meeting someone who called himself Jesus. What would they say to each other? Would there be jealousy? Would they become best friends? Would they join together? What effect would they have on each other? This bizarre scenario was about to unfold before my very eyes.

CHAPTER EIGHT

Sid G.

During this period, the residents of Rosewood began forming small groups with common interests, or common psyches. Jefferson was full of questions and admiration for Ludwig, and managed to persuade Jesus to produce a violin and viola so that they could play together. Adolph was beguiled by Joan, and offered to help sharpen the blade of her sword for the next battle against whatever infidel might come along. Jesus himself went around preaching to whoever would listen, but at that moment found little interest from the others in a discussion of his profound ideas.

German continued to be the *lingua franca*, and this put a strain on the staff, who had no way of knowing what was being said, which in turn delighted both Adolph and Ludwig.

*****

At 8:30 the next morning, an elderly, bald, pot-bellied man with a ridiculous smile on his face was led into the Rosewood office and introduced to staff. He wore a dark red robe and sandals, and said little as he surveyed the scene with wide-open, savvy eyes.

"Sid," said Director Nicholas, "I believe that you will find your new home to be comfortable."

"Yes," Sid replied with utter indifference.

As I led Sid into the Common Room, all the other patients were there. I introduced Sid to them one by one—Tom, Ludwig, Adolph, Joan, and Jesus. He gazed into the eyes of each one. When I came to Jesus, Sid's face lit up with an enormous grin. He then whispered "Namaste" to everyone, walked into the patio, assumed the lotus position near a rose bush, and went into meditation.

It's hard to describe the feeling that I and the others present had at that moment. It was as though a wave of calmness had just passed into our community, and was affecting our minds and emotions. Whatever our problems, be they physical, social, spiritual, or psychiatric, they seemed to grow smaller, to the point of insignificance. It wasn't that we agreed with this man's reported views, that we ought to just forget about our problems. It was more a sensation of just being in his presence—of looking into his soft eyes and being sucked in by that ridiculous smile. How could one feel anxiety when this little fat man deflected it with his joyful manner, even if he were absolutely crazy? Or maybe craziness was part of it, or at its center. Maybe one needed to be crazy to let go of life's many tensions. Yes, maybe that was it! This kind of craziness led to freedom from fear, and to unlimited joy.

Jesus was the most visibly moved. He couldn't stop staring at this man sitting next to the rose bush, with eyes closed and a body so relaxed that it seemed to be rising above the ground. In a hurried manner, Jesus came over to me and said, "Patrick, I must have a talk with Sid as soon as possible. Maybe something like what you did for Thomas and me, by the river. I need to understand his energy."

I told Jesus that I would do what I could, as soon as I could. But I was not about to awaken Sid from his current trance. Jesus, the Prince of Peace, would have to be patient.

And so it was that later that day, I arranged for the three of us—Jesus, Sid and me—to go for a drive to a place called Land's End, where we walked to a spectacular waterfall overlooking a large meadow. Jesus appeared not just excited, but almost ecstatic to be spending this time with Siddhartha. And Sid—he seemed disinterested in whatever or whoever might lay in his path. Fortunately, they both adhered to my request that they speak in English, not German, so that I could understand every word.

Once more, I wished that I could have captured this event on film, or at least on some kind of audiotape, for posterity. However such was not to be the case, so readers will have to accept this humble narrative, written later that day.

*****

61

While sitting on a mossy rock, Jesus began by asking a surprisingly direct question. "Siddhartha," he said in a soft but stressed tone, "when you look at me, what do you see?"

The Buddha said nothing for a time, as we had come to expect from this enigmatic creature. He just looked at Jesus' eyes, and at his body, which was healthy, but which was also shaking with fear, anxiety, or both.

"I see a man," he said at last, "who is holding on to vast burdens that make his life what one might call a living Hell."

Jesus winced at these words, and I thought *How odd that Jesus, who had recently told me about his vision of Hell, was now being told that he himself was living in something similar.*

After a long silence, Siddhartha whispered to him, "Am I right?"

Jesus nodded and then said, in a rising tone of anger, "Yes, Siddhartha. I love all humankind. And yes, I have endured terrible pain on the cross. And yes, I care deeply about what has happened, what is happening, and what will happen in the future to my people. Yes! Yes! Yes! And what you don't seem to understand is that you can't have love without pain! They go together! So you can take your God-Damned passionless views of life and stick them up your ass!"

Amazing! I knew from reading about his behavior with the money changers, that Jesus had a temper. But I never expected to witness this kind of language from him. And addressed, of all people, to The Buddha! I began to see Jesus as a man with levels of complexity which I had never dreamed of. Inside his heart there might be infinite love, but this was balanced by an angry, tempestuous side which stood in stark contrast to the calm Buddha at his side.

"Aah so," replied the Buddha calmly. One might even say coldly.

Jesus was looking sheepish now, knowing that he had humiliated himself before Buddha and me. I sensed that he would give almost anything to take back his last words. I also sensed that he wanted to continue this dialog to learn what he could from this totally different kind of pacifist.

"Siddhartha," he said softly, "please forgive me. I truly did not mean to speak to you in that way."

"Jesus," replied The Buddha, "there is nothing to forgive. You were just being you, and there is nothing wrong with that. Still, I should add that your clinging to suffering as a form of spirituality makes no sense to me."

"But Siddhartha, how can you remain so impassive when a baby is dying, when a woman is in pain during childbirth, or six million Jews are murdered in the Holocaust? Don't you, in some way, feel their pain? If you don't, you can't be human, and you certainly can't call yourself compassionate."

Siddhartha drew a big breath and waited some time before answering. "The human ego," he said at last, "is difficult to escape, particularly in the situations you mentioned. But who are we to question the way things are? Pain and suffering exist, the same as pleasure and joy. They, and other dimensions of good and evil, are all part of life, and we need to accept all of this if we are to be truly enlightened. Yes, we need acceptance of everything, along with compassion for all beings. You may say that these two are opposites, and are therefore incompatible. But I believe they can both be present at the same time. I try to manifest them both in my spirit, every second of every day. I know that you and other Christians see life differently, and that is fine with me."

"Buddha!" Jesus yelled, using Siddhartha's title for the first time, "Wake up! You're living in a lifeless bubble! Think of the pain which you caused your wife, Yosodhara, your son, Rahula, your father, Suddhoyana, and your mother, Maya, when you left them at the palace in Lumbini, never to return! Yes, you were on a mission to save mankind from suffering. But you also brought your family great pain! Can't you feel this? Don't you have an ounce of true feeling in your body, in your soul? Think, for once, of your own children!"

The great Buddha was clearly not used to being addressed in this manner. He closed his eyes, assumed the lotus position once again, and said nothing. Jesus and I watched this stoic figure as he evidently processed these words. Minutes went by, maybe an hour, maybe two. I lost track of time. Then, at last, came a sign. A small tear arose near the bottom of his left eye and dripped onto one of his legs. And another. And another. His obese body started shaking, and he wept. He wept! Imagine! The great Buddha, master of emotions, weeping.

Jesus went over to Buddha, put his arms around him, and held Buddha's head against his own. "Yes, Sid," he said. "It's all right. It's all right to feel pain, because this is a natural part of love, and of being human."

Buddha said nothing. He neither acknowledged the feeling of pain nor denied it. I got the feeling that he was being stubborn. Jesus' words had probed to the inner depths of Sid's soul. But no, Sid was not yet ready to give up detachment to all life, good and bad, joyful and painful.

Jesus broke the silence with these words. "Siddhartha, may I let you in on a little secret?"

Buddha said nothing, and Jesus went on anyway. "Ever since I learned about your life's mission to eliminate suffering, I have felt like you were a twin brother. Your approach is certainly different from mine, and it has nothing to do with my Lord. But it has brought a calmness and peace to so many people, and even to me, especially when I was on the cross. During that terrible time, I was comforted so much by you and your ideas! I truly love you!"

Buddha said nothing.

There was no conversation during our drive back home. Jesus had a kind of warm glow on his face, perhaps for having expressed his love to a very special person. And Buddha was still lost in a kind of enigmatic reflection. I was feeling uniquely privileged to have witnessed this day, but I also had a feeling of irresolution.

*****

When we walked through the front door to the Rosewood office. I noticed a new name on the board: Mike A. The fax documents were lying on my desk.

PATIENT: *Mike Angelo (alias Michelangelo di Lodovico Buonarroti Simoni)*

RECENT HISTORY: *Patient was found painting graffiti on the wall of a large public building in Ophir, California. The Ophir Police Department initially arrested him on charges of defacing public property and resisting arrest, but when others in their department arrived for backup, they determined that he was mentally ill and 5150ed him as gravely disabled. He was taken to Sutter Roseville Hospital for an assessment.*

BACKGROUND: *Patient claimed to have been born in Caprese, Italy in 1475. He said he was raised by a banking family in Florence where he studied anatomy, painting, and sculpture under some of the masters of the day. A series of political maneuvers involving the Medici family, several Popes in Rome, and other high-placed aristocrats, reportedly caused the patient to move to Venice, back to Florence, and then to the Italian capital of Rome, where he claims to have produced sculptures of Moses and The Pieta, and a painting called The Creation on the ceiling of the Sistine Chapel. He also believed that he died in 1564 of a slow fever in Rome, and that he had no idea how he came back to life in 2012.*

MEDICAL HISTORY: *Asperger's disorder, with symptoms of communication problems, repetitive behaviors, and a limited range of interests; post traumatic stress disorder due to severe physical abuse by his father during childhood*

PSYCHIATRIC DIAGNOSES: *Schizophrenia, with delusions; obsessive-compulsive personality disorder*

So how would such a figure, perhaps the greatest artist in human history, fit in with the rest of our cast of celebrities? We were about to find out.

*****

As a side note, you'll never guess what happened to me earlier today in the Common Room. Just as I was sitting down to eat breakfast, I felt someone tickling my ribs from behind. Yes, it was Joan, whose giggle persisted as I tried to stop laughing in this awkward posture. She was wearing an alluring red dress and sporting an impish smile that could dethrone an emperor.

CHAPTER NINE

Mike A.

The mood at Rosewood was tense during the rest of that day and night. I think it was mainly due to Siddhartha, who had earlier been such a calming presence, but who, after his tete-a-tete with Jesus, appeared to be in some kind of confused funk. He kept to his room and acknowledged no one when the staff made their hourly roster checks. Even though he was out of sight, the other residents sensed that something was wrong, and this was unsettling to us all.

From what I had been told about Buddhism, this funk should never have occurred. Buddhists—and particularly The Buddha—prided themselves on not becoming attached to anyone or anything in the world. They lived in a state of perpetual bliss in which they looked down on the rest of the world with a kind of disinterest, disapproval, or love, depending on one's point of view. In this case, Jesus had evidently said something to shake the very foundation of Sid's *persona*. It may well have been the reference to each member of Sid's family, whom Sid had indeed abandoned at an early age.

Meanwhile, Jesus seemed almost as confused as Siddhartha. Feeling directly responsible for this new and unexpected mood disorder, Jesus wanted to help Sid in some way, but Sid was not talking to anyone. The funk would have to be left to fester for a while.

*****

At 8:30 the next morning, a muscular full-bearded man, about 6 feet tall and weighing around 230 pounds, was escorted into the Rosewood office by one social worker and three policemen. There was fire and impatience in his eyes. He was carrying with him two very old wooden boxes—one with different kinds of paint brushes, and the other with a variety of hammers and chisels. When introduced to us, he paid no attention to the Rosewood staff or other residents. Instead, he looked up at the walls and ceiling of the dining room, and then out at the garden patio. Then he shouted some exclamation in Italian.

"Does anyone here understand what our new resident has just said?" I asked.

"Yes, I do," Tom replied. "He is asking for, or, should I say, demanding, a number of oil paints to do some kind of work on the walls and ceiling around us. He is also demanding a 10' by 8' by 6' block of white marble from the town of Carrara in Italy, to be delivered immediately to the outside patio."

This was greeted with laughter from some of the other residents, who thought such requests to be fanciful and unrealistic. Upon hearing this laughter, Mike broke into a scathing verbal attack of them in Italian, which, perhaps thankfully, almost no one in our group could understand.

Jesus came to the aid of our latest resident, but this time his aid had no verbal component. Instead, he simply waved his arms and produced, inside the dining room, twenty-five large cans of paint. Outside, in the patio, he produced a rough block of white marble of the requested description. There was a stunned silence by everyone except for Mike, who yelled, "Santo Espirito, Vittorio Por Fin!"

*****

Life, I have noticed through the years, does not always conduct itself in a linear fashion. And thus it was with Mike's obsessive need to paint and sculpt. Nicholas dutifully reported Rosewood's latest curious episode to the Glacier County Mental Health authorities and asked that this new resident be allowed to create. They, in turn, summarily dismissed this request as a violation of county rules. The Director of our Mental Health Division, a certain Mr. Dalrumple, who was known for his small stature, bow ties, and Napoleonic temper, appeared in person within the hour to exercise his authority in this matter. Having heard that there might be trouble, he came accompanied by three members of the Roseville Police Department.

"Gentlemen," he announced in a firm voice to all Rosewood residents and staff, "and ladies." He paused.

"There is no way that such a large art project can possibly be tolerated within the confines of our Rosewood facility. I am afraid that I shall have to put such ideas to rest here and now. Police, please load the cans of paint onto the dollies I instructed you to bring, and remove this ugly rock from the premises!"

This precipitated an outburst of angry Italian words from Mike, directed at Mr. Dalrumple.

"What's he saying?" came Dalrumple's reply.

Tom translated. "Mr. Angelo says that he has been waiting several centuries to use his skills both as a painter and a sculptor. Now that at last this opportunity has arisen, he is not inclined to be turned away by some petty bureaucrat. In times past, he has stood up to Popes and to members in high standing of the Medici family. And he is ready to do whatever it takes to thrust aside this tiny—I'm afraid, Sir, I cannot give an appropriate translation of the name he just called you."

"Very well," said Mr. Dalrumple in an unyielding tone, "then I shall again command the members of our Roseville Police Department to remove these paint cans immediately, and to smash this marble block into pieces small enough to be hauled away. If anyone, in particular Mr. Angelo, tries to impede this order, he shall be arrested and will spend the rest of the night in jail. Do I make myself clear?"

Once again, I was struck by how the forces of our modern institutional world were coming into conflict with the forces of a mysterious historical world which I had not begun to understand. At that moment I could swear that I saw Jesus, for a small fraction of a second, give Mike a wink.

And so it was that when the policemen tried to pick up the paint cans and put them on the dollies, they were unable to do so. And when they tried to use their hammers, and later, sledge hammers, and later, jackhammers, to break the marble into smaller pieces, they were unable to do this as well.

Meanwhile, Mr. Dalrumple was watching all this with increasing annoyance. "Look, boys," he said to the embarrassed Roseville policemen, "when I was in the Army, we used to destroy *tanks* in ten seconds. It's just a question of motivation and training."

"All right," said the Captain in charge, clearly miffed. He passed the jackhammer on to Mr. Dalrumple and said, "Then *you* do it!"

"Boys," said the determined Director of Glacier County Mental Health, "for big jobs, you've got to use big equipment." He grabbed a submachine gun from one of the officers standing by, and pointed it directly at the mass of stubborn marble.

"No, wait!" yelled the police captain. There were other cries of "It's too risky!" and "The ricochets! Watch out for the ricochets!"

But the gallant Mental Health Director was not about to be deterred when the pride of the United States Army was on the line. "BAM-BAM-BAM-BAM-BAM-BAM-BAM! BAM-BAM-BAM-BAM-BAM!" The very loud submachine gun smashed its bullets directly into the marble block and made no dent whatsoever. The shots bounced off of it and careened into the walls and ceiling of our dining room. Incredibly, no one was hurt.

Then, in an unleashed fury, Mr. Dalrumple aimed and fired the submachine gun at Mr. Angelo himself. When this produced no effect, he aimed it at the Police Chief, who finally charged Mr. Dalrumple, knocked him over, and yelled, "Sir, you're under arrest!"

Handcuffs had soon locked the Director's hands behind his back.

"You have the right to remain silent, Sir! And you will be allowed to make a phone call and obtain legal representation just as soon as we get you to the Roseville Jail!"

The rest of us stood there in a daze. We had almost forgotten that this episode had started with an insistent Mike crying out for tools, and Jesus, miraculously, producing them. Then came the Roseville Police, and Dalrumple's strange behavior. I looked around again at the cast of characters: Jesus, Buddha, Jefferson, Hitler, Mike, Ludwig, Joan. *Was this all real? Or was I only*

71

dreaming, or going crazy?

*****

Perhaps this is a good time to mention that Glacier County Mental Health has always had a protective coating of secrecy around its activities. The stated purpose was confidentiality, encoded in what is known in California as the HIPPA Act. An unstated purpose was to protect the county against lawsuits of any kind. Another purpose, also never stated but always well known by those on the inside, was to cover up anything which might prove embarrassing to the power structure of Glacier County's top management.

And so it was that not a word about Director Dalrumple's criminal behavior and subsequent arrest was leaked to the press. Indeed, after several tightly-controlled phone calls to high places (and no written memos), Mr. Dalrumple was released from jail and allowed to continue as Glacier County Mental Health Director, with nothing changed.

*****

The next morning, at 9:45 am, the Rosewood office received notice of a new patient. We dutifully wrote down the first name and first initial of the last name on our increasingly crowded board: "Eleanor R." Fifteen minutes later, we received a fax with this discharge summary:

PATIENT: *Eleanor Roosevelt (alias Anna Eleanor Roosevelt, alias First Lady Eleanor Roosevelt)*

RECENT HISTORY: *Patient is a white female, 5' 11 tall, 170 pounds, and appearing to be in her mid-70s. She was found on a rainy night at the Wayside Shelter for the Homeless, trying to help people who had been turned away due to their unsuitable alcoholic or drug conditions. When the manager of the shelter tried to explain the reason why such clients could not be served, she became furious and threatened to call the President of the United States. When the Police were called, she was 5150ed to Sutter Roseville Hospital on a charge of grave disability. The next day she was sent to the Rosewood Psychiatric Facility.*

The patient continually stated that there was no reason why America, with all of its wealth and a Christian heritage, should be turning away poor addicts from a homeless shelter on a cold, rainy night. Her views were expressed in an increasingly belligerent tone, which at one point required restraint from the hospital staff.

BACKGROUND: *Patient claims to have been born in 1884 into a distinguished family in New York City. Her parents and her brother, Elliot, died before she was 11, and she was raised by a strict maternal grandmother. She grew up feeling ugly and starved for affection. After being sent to a finishing school out-side London at the age of 15, she began to gain self-esteem and to become concerned with such causes as women's rights, racial discrimination, and helping the poor.*

Patient claims that her Uncle Teddy (Roosevelt) was the 26th President of the United States, and that in 1905 he married her to the eventual 32nd president, cousin Franklin Roosevelt. She also claimed that in spite of a mostly loveless marriage, she led a fulfilling life helping people in need. She reported her greatest accomplishment to be developing the United Nations Universal Declaration of Human Rights.

MEDICAL HISTORY: *Aplastic anemia; bone marrow tuber culosis*

PSYCHIATRIC DIAGNOSIS: *Intermittent episodes of mild de-pression and anxiety, delusions of grandeur, and low self-esteem.*

*****

73

Inside the staff room, we had a long discussion about what was happening to our facility and to our lives. My buddy Craig reached into his literary background and likened our situation to that of *Marat Sade*, the story of an asylum during the time of the French Revolution. Tawny (the woman looking for a good man), likened it to *Alice in Wonderland*, where we had all fallen down a rabbit hole and into a world which was getting "curiouser and curiouser." I likened it to my experience in Vietnam, where everything seemed to be upside down—our country fighting against freedom and democracy in a fit of highly destructive, drug-infested, ethnocentrism.

Director Nicholas, always sweet and sensitive, reminded us that whatever was happening here at Rosewood needed to kept totally secret from the outside world. "What happens at Rosewood," he said with a smile, "stays at Rosewood."

Part of our problem was that most of our patients didn't speak English. Up to now, Jesus, Jefferson, and Buddha were the only ones with whom the staff could converse comfortably, and none of these three had any interest in mental health. Another part of our problem was that without exception, our patients all appeared to be bigger than life in their personalities. In their minds, they were all celebrities in their own strange worlds and, as such, accustomed to privilege and power. They had little respect for social work peons like us, and had almost no awareness of their own mental health challenges. Not one of them was taking their prescribed medications—their right to refuse under California law. And without their taking medications or undergoing therapeutic treatment, our jobs had become relegated to that of attendants, or, as we called it, babysitting.

We were pleased to hear that our next guest could speak English, and that she claimed to have an interest in helping people in need. But we were also feeling intimidated, for the real Eleanor Roosevelt was widely recognized as the greatest woman of the twentieth century.

*****

74

"Another woman?" Brigit exclaimed when I got home. "What's she like?"

"Well," I said, "she's a crusader for the rights of all oppressed people. She's very nice, and she's around eighty years old."

"I like the young one better."

CHAPTER TEN

Eleanor R.

Patterns were emerging at Rosewood as our census reached seven and was stretching toward eight. As in times past, there were a couple of residents (Adolph and Joan) who remained withdrawn. They stayed in their rooms most of the day, and came to the common room only for meals. They seldom engaged in conversation with anyone, even though most of the other residents spoke some German or French. Sid was also withdrawn, although some might call his behavior spiritual.

Also as in times past, there were a couple of residents who threw themselves totally into activities. Ludwig had a corner of the garden where he was working hard on a new musical composition. The grand piano had been removed by Jesus, and in its place a smaller harpsichord had been produced for greater convenience. Occasionally we would be treated to a little riff, which was played with great care, sometimes over and over. Our staff puzzled over his reputed deafness, for it seemed like he could hear the notes of his harpsichord quite well, and his recent outburst toward Adolph had opened up the possibility that his handicap was mostly psychological.

Mike had a favorite table in the patio where he was working away at drawings which would presumably be turned later into larger works of art. Every so often, he would pull out a paintbrush and test certain colors, or pick up a chisel and chop a few flakes off of the large white marble in the patio. Inspired perhaps by the intriguing characters around him, he had decided to turn the walls and ceiling of the Common Room into a 12-panel production called *Rosewoodians*. Finding a theme for the large sculpture was more difficult, although Jesus suggested that it depict John the Baptist and Jefferson thought that it might be nice to do something with Noah's Ark.

It should be noted that Jesus and Jefferson were quite different from the rest of our current residents. They were more gregarious, and they spent hours together talking about all sorts of things, from the true nature of man and woman, to humankind's seemingly constant need for war. But in spite of their rapport with each other, there was also a common frustration.

Each of them wanted to engage directly in the planetary affairs of the present day, and Rosewood was clearly not the place to do this. More and more, I was to overhear them mention the word, escape.

*****

At 4:15 pm, or tea time, as our next resident would call it, a tall, ungainly, white woman of about 70, dressed in a fashionable gray suit and matching hat from the 1940s, was escorted into our office by a young Latina social worker. They were chatting away in Spanish and having what this next resident called "a marvelous time."

Upon entering our quarters, the tall woman flashed a broad smile and said in a squeaky, high-pitched voice, "Hello, my name is Eleanor, and to whom do I have the pleasure of meeting at this point in my day?" She looked exactly like the pictures which I had seen.

There were smiles all around as a beaming Nicholas replied, "Welcome to Rosewood, Mrs. Roosevelt. Our new home is not as comfortable as the one you may be accustomed to in Campobello, but I think you'll find our company to be both friendly and interesting."

"Yes, indeed, "she replied, "the pleasure is all mine."

We went through the formalities of introduction and the inventory of her many possessions. She had brought five large suitcases and three hat boxes. The clothes were all early twentieth century, and there were a number of books and letters. When we mentioned Rosewood's limit of two bags per resident, she laughed and said, "Yes, by all means. Throw them all away! After all, you can only wear one outfit at a time."

As Eleanor walked into the Common Room, I noticed that most of its current residents were there. Jesus and Jefferson were at one table, Ludwig at another, and Mike at another. Adolph was leaning against a door in the hall.

"Ladies and gentlemen," said a smiling Nicholas, "It is my

pleasure to introduce to you our newest resident, Eleanor Roosevelt. We hope you will all make her feel at home."

It took Adolph all of about three seconds to register this new name and the figure in front of him before he lunged at her with a plastic knife picked up from the snack table. And it was only one more second before he fell to the floor in front of Eleanor in a state of catatonic paralysis.

"Goodness!" Eleanor yelled, as she stepped back, safely out of the way. "Is he all right? We must get him to a hospital fast! The poor creature!"

I realized my lack of foresight. Such a scene was likely to occur, since Adolph would recognize her husband as the leader of the enemy that he had fought for four long years. When I explained to Eleanor that this man truly believed he was Adolph Hitler, her response was, "Poor baby! The suffering he must endure every day!" Then she wrinkled her brow and said to all who were there, "I will make it my mission to help this poor man for as long as I am here!"

Adolph was taken by ambulance to the Sutter Roseville Hospital, where he recovered fully in a short time. He was back at Rosewood the next morning, where he stayed in his room.

Meanwhile, it was my job to make Eleanor feel comfortable at Rosewood. I told her that she would be sharing a room with another suffering person, this one believing that she was Joan of Arc and had been burned at the stake in the fifteenth century. "Well then," said Eleanor, "since I speak some French, I shall try to help her too."

Eleanor showed less interest in the other residents. Ludwig and Mike were clearly in their own worlds, which she was content to ignore. She showed no interest in Siddhartha. Jesus and Jefferson might as well have been Joe Shmoe and Harry Schwartz, for all she cared.

Later in the evening, she overheard Jesus and Tom talk about escaping from Rosewood, and she said to them, "Well, why don't you just ask the Director here if you can leave. Maybe he'll say yes."

Then, in a take-charge manner which I was beginning to observe, she went one step farther. She knocked on Nicholas' door, asked him to come to the Common Room, and said to Nicholas for all to hear, "These two gentlemen have told me that they would like to leave Rosewood now. Would that be all right with you?"

Nicholas looked at this outspoken new resident with a degree of admiration, and then at Jesus and Jefferson. "It's fine with me. As long as residents are not currently on a 5150 hold, and have a viable plan for food, shelter, and safety, they can leave at any time. "

Tom and Jesus looked at each other, and Tom said, "I think Jesus and I need to talk this over. We'll get back to you soon."

"Fine."

Nicholas returned to his room, Eleanor attended to Joan, and Tom and Jesus began talking about their future while I eavesdropped from across the room. Since neither of them had any support on the outside, financial or otherwise, and since they now knew that they were not prisoners and could leave Rosewood at any time, they decided to stay a while.

Eleanor re-entered the room and the conversation. "I sense that you two are getting antsy about this place," she said. "Maybe you both need a change of scene, like a vacation or something, or maybe a short trip."

It was my turn to propose that Tom and Jesus join me for an overnight camping trip. "I know a nice place on the North Fork of the American River. It's a short hike from the road, and few people know about it. I'm pretty sure that Nicholas will let me take you there."

"Well, if they're going," said Eleanor, "then I'd like to go, too. I've only been here a few hours, but you already know me. I'm, uh, well, I guess you might call me assertive, but also easy-going."

At that moment, Buddha popped his head in the Common Room doorway leading to the outside hall. He said, "Count me in, too."

81

A few minutes later, I knocked on Nicholas' door, told him my proposal, and asked if it would be okay.

He pondered the notion for a moment, and then said, "Patrick, I trust you. But frankly this proposal would never fly with upper management. I'll let you go on one condition—that neither you nor any of the other participants say a word about this to anyone. Do you understand?"

"Yes, Sir." Then I added, "You've always been my model of the perfect supervisor."

"Well, I don't know about that," he mumbled. "By the way, where're you going?"

"Hell's Canyon."

CHAPTER ELEVEN

Hell's Canyon

I don't know how Hell's Canyon got its name. It might have been from a steep, slippery stretch of trail on the way down. It could also have been from the many bears who seemed to enjoy congregating there at night, or the mosquitoes, which were annoying during the last two months of summer. As an avid hiker, none of these things bothered me much, and I rather liked the fact that this negative reputation was keeping the crowds away.

Perhaps because I'd done this kind of thing many times before, I was able to round up five packs and sleeping bags, cooking equipment, and two large rainproof tents. Brigit and I worked together to make sandwiches for lunch, cereal and eggs for breakfast, and a surprise dinner.

It was around 9 a.m. when our party of five squeezed into my metallic green Subaru Outback and left for the wilderness. Eleanor, as the only woman, was given the preferred passenger seat to my right. Behind me, from right to left, were Jefferson, Buddha and Jesus. Although Buddha had the largest girth of the three, he was also the shortest, and we decided that he would be the least uncomfortable in the middle. While the rest of us had somewhat normal hiking clothes, Buddha insisted on wearing one of his orange robes, and I warned him that this might cause him to trip on the trail.

"No problem," he muttered as he squeezed into my car. I would say that as we left Rosewood that morning, the general mood was both calm and a bit excited.

"You know," Eleanor told me as we turned onto Interstate 80, "when I was a child, my greatest hero was Uncle Teddy, who was not only President, but who loved adventuring in the wilderness. He often told me how much he enjoyed the camping trip he took into Yosemite with the naturalist, John Muir. I guess they saw lots of bears and wolves and other creatures. I feel a little like that now."

The road passed through a dense forest of pines and firs, and then past a stretch where a fire had decimated all vegetation several years ago. In the distance were some of the snow-capped peaks of the Sierra Nevada; Mt. Lincoln, Tinker's Knob, and

Squaw Peak among them. Thunderclouds threatened overhead, but my group didn't seem to mind. This was a welcome change from the cramped quarters of Rosewood.

A flashing red light from behind interrupted my reverie, and a motorcycle cop pulled me over to give me a ticket.

"Sorry, officer," I said. "I guess I wasn't paying much attention to my speed."

"No you weren't," he replied coldly. From the back seat, I noticed grins coming from both Buddha and Jesus, who weren't about to intervene on my behalf.

"Is this your family?" the policeman asked.

"Well, uh, yes, I guess they are, in a way," I answered.

"Better keep an eye on him," he told them.

They replied, "Yes sir," and my mood sunk to a new low.

After the policeman left, we continued on I-80 east, toward Castle Peak on the left, and the South Fork of the Yuba River on the right. Large groves of yellow aspen trees were in all their glory. And then it started.

A small whiff, at first, barely noticeable. My mind tried to persuade my nose that it wasn't real, the faint smell of excrement in a crowded car.

But then it grew stronger. And stronger. No one said anything, but I'm sure everyone smelled it. It was hard to ignore. Time passed, and there was a kind of loaded silence.

I wasn't sure how to handle this one. To begin with, I didn't know who the culprit was. I didn't think it was Eleanor, because the smell didn't seem to be coming from my right. No, it was definitely coming from the back seat. Was it Jesus, Buddha, or Jefferson? Having some experience with each of their personalities, none of them seemed like good candidates.

We drove on for another ten minutes, until finally Jesus reported, "I'm terribly sorry, but I seemed to have had an accident."

Nothing more needed to be said. I pulled the car onto a wooded turnout and told him, "I have an extra change of clothes, and you seem to be about my size. Why don't you take these and change behind that group of trees? Here's a garbage bag to put your clothes in, and some rags and a roll of toilet paper. We'll wait here until you're finished."

"I'm so sorry!" he said, very embarrassed.

Then Buddha burst into laughter and said, "Jesus, I'm so glad this happened! It means you're one of us! I could just kiss you! Muuaa!" He blew a little kiss in Jesus' direction.

Jesus gave Buddha a long look, mostly of annoyance, but at the end of it there was a barely perceptible smile.

Soon, a cleaner Jesus was back in the car, and we drove on toward the turn-off to Hell's Canyon. The dirt road at the turn-off was full of potholes, fallen rocks, and newly eroded ditches. My little Subaru was not made for this kind of travel, so I went slowly. At one point I had to decide whether or not to pass over a large rock stuck in the middle of the road. I did, ever so slowly, and rubbed the oil pan beneath my car in the process, but there was no major damage.

There were no other vehicles at the trail-head—just a meadow with a small stream, fallen trees, and ponds probably teeming with trout. The packs had already been arranged to distribute the weight equally, and we adjusted the straps to our respective sizes. A mixture of sunlight and white thunderclouds looked down on us as we began our trek along a pleasant trail. The downward slope was gradual at first, and then became steeper. Eleanor was exuberant, but no one else talked, and eventually she, too, became quiet. The scenery was beautiful, but there was some other strange energy in our midst. I felt like we were being watched by ancient gods.

When we came to the very steep spot which I remembered, I noticed that it was muddier than usual and part of the trail had fallen away. It was much more narrow, slippery, and dangerous than before. There was no way to see the ground on the downward side of the trail, but one might guess that it was several hundred feet away. No one could survive a fall like that.

"Are there any other routes that go around this stretch?" asked the ever-resourceful Eleanor.

"Nope."

86

"Do you think we should turn back?" asked Jefferson.

"Nope," answered Buddha, mimicking me with a smile. "I think it's our *dharma* to walk over this trail, or die."

"Well then," said Eleanor, "at my age, I feel that I have nothing to lose. Here we go." She walked directly across the narrow trail, always looking ahead, and only slipping once.

At the other side, she called back, "If I can do it, than I would think that the males of our species can do it, too."

Next came Jefferson, who showed remarkable agility for a man of his advanced age.

Sid, or Buddha, was third. As he started, he said, "The ninth incarnation of Vishnu should have nothing to fear." But as he spoke the word "fear," he tripped on his orange robe and began to plummet downward toward whatever hellish future awaited him below.

As it turned out, Jesus was the next in line behind Buddha, and he foresaw the tragedy unfolding in front of him. He reached out with his right hand and grabbed the left hand of Buddha, barely in time. The immense torso of the Buddha swung directly beneath him, as Jesus struggled to gain a footing to hold the great weight. I reached my own right hand toward Jesus to give added support.

Buddha's body went limp! There was no sign of muscle movement whatsoever, as it appeared that he might have lost consciousness. Cries of "Sid, wake up!" and "Hold on, Buddha!" came from the other members of our group in this life-or-death situation.

Somehow, Jesus held on to Buddha by grabbing a tree root and positioning his feet on a secure piece of the ledge. While I tried to support Jesus by holding his left arm with my right, Tom and Eleanor both came back across the dangerous ledge to help, but the trail was too steep.

As the four of us struggled to secure our position. Buddha appeared to regain consciousness. His eyes opened, and an expression of utter calm came over his face. "Jesus," he said, "please don't worry about me. If I fall and die, so be it. It's my *dharma.*"

"To Hell with your God-Damned *dharma!*" Jesus screamed. "We can do it! Just be calm and we'll have you up here in no time!"

"Jesus!" cried Jefferson, "Use your gifts! Bring him up with your magic powers!"

"I can't!" Jesus replied, in a helpless tone.

At that point, the muddy ledge Jesus had been bracing himself on gave way. Jesus had no choice but to let go of Buddha's hand, and Buddha plummeted down the cliff and out of sight.

"Nooo!" Jesus cried as he watched Buddha fall. "I'm sorry! I couldn't hold you anymore! I'll love you forever, my dear one! Please forgive me!"

Then there was silence.

The remaining four of us stood there on that ledge, looking downward in disbelief, each with our own thoughts passing through our minds. I'll be honest here. I hadn't developed much of a relationship with Buddha, so I didn't really care that much that he had disappeared from my life. But the consequences! Oh, the consequences! For a start, I would immediately be fired from my job, and so would poor Nicholas—and Rosewood would be shut down pending an investigation. And all these amazing clients would be dispersed into other facilities. *I had been such an idiot!*

A thousand images flooded my mind as I stood, traumatized, on that muddy ledge...*the flashing red and blue lights of police cars, helicopters and other rescue vehicles... the lifeless body of the man who called himself Buddha being hauled out of the canyon on a blanketed stretcher! The look of guilt and horror in Jesus' eyes, as if he hadn't suffered enough, the pained faces of Jefferson and Eleanor, and then... Coming home to explain all this to poor Brigit. Seven-year-old little Brigit shouldn't have to suffer this shame to her father. No child should. What would I tell her? And what would I tell a judge? Surely there would be charges of criminal negligence. And what would be my defense? Nothing!*

As my mind became more delirious, my body became more faint. *How could I face all these consequences of the stupidest thing I had ever done? Was life worth living any more, with nothing but shame and misery ahead?*

Slowly, my legs began to buckle. My brain lost all control, and my body slipped over the edge of that same muddy cliff. With nothing but pain and suffering to look forward to, I didn't care.

Then my mind stepped into the world of my past—*memories of people and other living creatures I had known...a sixteen-year-old Vietnamese boy in Phan Rang who came to ask me if he should join the corrupt Vietnamese Army or the Viet Cong...a Kampa farmer in Tanzania who insisted on giving me his last worldly possession, a live chicken...a bully roommate at a Swiss school who stole my stamp collection and then beat me up... the many soccer goals I had scored at Stanford...the mountain gorilla in Rwanda who had stood up and pounded his chest just five feet away...and the day when I came into Brigit's life, and the long hug she gave me when she first saw me, with open arms. Oh my God!*

Then I mused that *I had lived many great years, and really had no regrets. And following Buddha into the Great Abyss might not be a bad way to end it all.*

*****

The next thing I knew, I was hanging upside down with a powerful hand holding me by my right ankle. Jesus again! I looked up at this bearded figure, feeling helpless, and hearing his soothing voice, "Patrick, *you're* not getting away, so help me God!"

Then another hand grabbed my left foot, and, in a series of jerks, I was being pulled up the cliff and over to a patch of ground where I could lie down in safety. But the joy of being alive was soon overcome by the reality that my life was forever ruined.

"I don't want to live!" I cried out. "Let me die and be rid of all my problems!" But these three saviors would have none of it.

"Like it or not," said Jesus, "We love you, and you are going to join us in whatever lies ahead!"

Now that sounded good, until I thought again about the upcoming trial, and all the shame that I had just brought upon my family and colleagues at work. Taking no chances, the three of them held me down, so that I had no opportunity to drop off the cliff again. In a strange way, it was reassuring, for it took that weighty decision out of my hands.

$$*****$$

Out of the distant southern sky, it appeared first as a speck of light. It could have been an airplane, a spacecraft, or a reflection off some kind of cloud. As it grew brighter, it seemed to be coming toward us, and the four of us observed it as one.

As it came closer, it was revealed as a fluttering object. At last, it came to within a few feet of us, and hovered in the air just off of the cliff. It was a large, white dove. And then, instantly, it morphed into an orange life-sized figure in the lotus position, with eyes closed, our Buddha!

His eyes opened into a light smile, and he said, "You didn't think that you could get rid of me that easily!" He stepped back onto the trail from which he had fallen, and danced a French can-can on that very stretch, while singing the corresponding tune, "Da-da-da-da-da-da-da-da-da-da-da-da-da-da-da-da-da-da-da Da-da-da-da-da-da-da..."

On and on it went, until at last Eleanor joined him, singing and dancing, and then Jefferson, and then Jesus, and finally, me! So there we were—all five of us dancing the can-can on this treacherous stretch of the Hell's Canyon trail, and feeling a joy which can only come from the catharsis of release from a dire tragedy.

Da-da, da-da-da-da, da-da-da-da-da-da da-da, da-da-da-da-da-da-da-da, da-da, da-da-da-da-da, da, da-da-da-da-da-da..."

At last, after this little suspension in time from the real world, we made our way down to a series of waterfalls on the North Fork of the American River. All five of us were elated, but there was something special going on between Buddha and Jesus. "I'll bet you can't walk on water across that pool!" Buddha said in a teasing tone to Jesus. (And Jesus did!)

"And I'll bet you can't turn yourself into a snake, and back again!" said Jesus. (And Buddha did!)

These kind of antics continued for a while, until I announced that dinner was ready. Brigit and I had prepared the meal which was most desired for each person. For Eleanor it was Welsh rarebit with mashed potatoes and Yorkshire pudding. For Jefferson it was *canard de l'orange* with *escargots* and lemon pastries. For Jesus it was a lamb stew with lentils and strawberries. For Buddha it was Portobello mushrooms with avocados and assorted fruit. And for me it was roast beef with corn on the cob and chocolate cake.

"Jesus," said Eleanor with an impish grin, "is it true that you can produce fish from nothing? I was thinking that a taste of king salmon with Hollandaise sauce might be nice." And this was produced almost as fast as the request was made!

As we settled down to some serious marshmallow roasting around a campfire, we heard the heavy growl of a nearby bear. Normally this would have induced some kind of fear in me, and I would have hastened to batten down the food hatches and headed for my tent. But not this time. In this fairyland of amazing characters, I saw Buddha instantly transform himself into the largest black bear I had ever seen. His enormous growl appeared to attract the attention of all the other bears of the neighborhood, and we soon had more than fifteen of them standing on all fours around our campfire. Buddha led them all in a bizarre kind of can-can dance around the fire, and of course, the other four of us joined in.

The mixture of our "da, da, da-da-da-da-da-da's", with the bears' "arrgh, arrgh, arrgh-arrgh-aargh-aargh-aargh-aargh"'s was so bizarre that every creature there seemed to have a good laugh, and a couple of the bears actually fell over on their backs in what appeared to be some kind of hysterics! It lasted a while, until at last Buddha changed back into his human form and the bears went off to do whatever bears do in the woods.

The rest of the evening was spent telling stories, some true, some not true, but nobody cared. I won't bore readers with a chronicle of all the details, but I will mention that at one point in the evening someone asked if each of us would describe a difficult decision in our lives. For Eleanor, it came after discovering her husband's infidelity with a secretary. She had to choose between staying in the marriage or not, and she chose to stay in the marriage for humanitarian reasons, because in that position she could help a lot of needy people.

Jefferson cited two difficult decisions. He started off with the purchase of the Louisiana Territory, which was great for the country but completely against his principles of self-determination, since the Indians and other residents of this territory had no say in this purchase whatsoever. Jefferson's second most difficult decision was whether or not to mortgage his slaves. This financial maneuver was the only way that he could keep his beloved Monticello, but it came at the price of human bondage for some of his closest friends.

"My own difficult moment," Buddha told us, "was the one which Jesus pointed out to me a short time ago. When I left my palace at Lumbini to search for an end to all suffering, I felt anxiety and shame, as well as a sense of purpose. For I was violating the trust of those who loved me most, and whom I loved the most. Ironically, my noble pursuit caused them all enormous pain—the very thing I was trying to end. Was my decision the right one? To this day, I can't be sure."

Jesus was next. "My most difficult decision came on the night following what people later came to call The Last Supper. Mary Magdalene came to me, and told me that she had arranged for the two of us to slip away from Jerusalem to a place where we would never be found. She argued that the world would be much better off with me alive than dead, and she pleaded with me not to put her, my family, and so many others, through this unnecessary agony. What purpose would it serve? For some reason, I made the decision not to escape. Like Buddha, I'm not sure to this day whether that was the right decision."

Then came my turn. Good grief! Can you imagine having to follow these four with my own mundane little speech? "Good friends," I told them modestly, "I hardly think that my own story merits a place in this rich discussion, but I'll tell it anyway. For me, it was the decision to leave a life of adventure, and come to the small town of Auburn to raise my darling daughter. I don't think I'll ever regret this decision, but I often yearn for the excitement of other cultures and major world causes to fight for."

At last, our fire was burning low, and my anti-climactic statement may have reminded the others of the importance of sleep. It had been a long day, and we all slipped into our respective tents and sleeping bags, and invoked the nocturnal spirits of yet another mysterious world.

In the morning, after a breakfast of cereal, bacon, and pancakes, we packed up and headed back to the upper world. As we left, Tom gave this admonition, "For many reasons, all that happened on this trip should forever remain a secret between the five of us."

And here I am, blurting it out now in book form, for all to read. Oh well, as the saying goes, "No one's perfect."

CHAPTER TWELVE

Bertie W.

When we got back to Rosewood, I was still worried that something about our trip might leak out and get me in trouble. But that didn't happen. The truth was that the other residents and staff had no interest whatsoever in where we had been. Besides, the Rosewood staff had something new to worry about—a rumor that our facility was likely to close in a few weeks, and that all of us would soon be out of a job!

There was also some discussion about two holidays which were fast approaching, Thanksgiving and Christmas. A candle-light feast with all of these historic figures was something I was not about to miss. And then Christmas! *Good grief*, I thought, *how often does one get to celebrate Jesus' birthday with the man himself?*

*****

A temporary distraction from these thoughts came from a phone call and fax describing our next resident.

PATIENT: *Bertie Wells (alias Herbert George Wells, alias H.G. Wells)*

RECENT HISTORY: *Patient is a white male, 5' 6" tall, 165 lbs., around 65 years of age, with a bushy moustache. He was found in the Roseville Library after hours, sitting at one of the computers and grumbling about how the world had changed. When asked to leave, he refused and said, "I have no interest in the rules of your corrupt society." He was restrained, 5150ed as gravely disabled, and taken to the Sutter Roseville Hospital.*

BACKGROUND: *Patient claimed he was born in 1866 to an impoverished family in Bromley, England. His father was a struggling shopkeeper and low-level cricketeer, and his moth-er a domestic servant. At the age of seven, he had an accident which left him bedridden for months and allowed him time to read many books which his father brought him from the local*

96

library. After failing as a draper's apprentice and a chemist's assistant, he was given an opportunity to study and then teach at the Morley Commercial Academy.

He claimed to have a curious mind, which over the course of his life, had delved into the writing of history, the natural and social sciences, and science fiction. He claimed to have pub-lished over 200 books, among them, An Outline of History *(the planet's best-seller in 1922),* The Science of Life, The Work, Wealth and Happiness of Mankind, *and* The Time Machine. *In most of his books and his thinking was a passionate regard for one world government, and for the welfare of the human race. He considered himself to be a free-thinker, where philandering with such notables as Rebecca West and Margaret Sanger, and challenging the nationalistic views of the leaders of his day, were an unabashed part of his lifestyle. He claimed to have died in 1946, in an atomic era in which "our species' weaponry ap-peared to have advanced far beyond our common sense."*

After being cleared by the Sutter Roseville Hospital, he was sent to the Rosewood Psychiatric Facility for further treatment and observation.

MEDICAL HISTORY: *Type II diabetes and onset of liver cancer*

PSYCHIATRIC DIAGNOSES: *Schizoaffective, with delusions of grandeur, borderline personality, and no support from family or friends*

It was 10:15 am when a tired, slouching, balding figure of a man was led into the office of our facility by a rather attractive young female social worker wearing a tight purple silk blouse. Our new resident's eyes remained fixed on the outline of the social worker's breasts while our director Nicholas introduced our staff. Eventually our new resident glanced over at the board with the other residents' names.

"Holy crap!" he said, as he saw the names of Adolph H., Jesus C., and the others. "Where am I? Is this a dream, a nut house, or some kind of joke?"

"This is a mental health facility," said Nicholas, calmly, as if there was nothing unusual about the names. "We're here to help you."

"Holy crap!" Bertie answered again. "You can't be serious! I feel like I've become a character in one of my novels. Well anyway, I'm very interested. Please introduce me to the other residents." His tired manner had disappeared, and he was bristling with energy.

As we walked into the common room, the first person he saw was Adolph. "Mein Herr," Bertie said, and then in perfect German (as was later translated to me), "the last time we met was at the Hofbrauhaus in Munich, over several pints of beer. You were with Goering, Himmler, and Speer, as I recall, and that lovable Irish setter."

Adolph, for the first time during his entire stay at Rosewood, broke into a grin, and walked over to give Bertie a big hug. The two men chattered away in German, and I'm told that Bertie said, "I told you so. That invasion of Poland and then Russia were the dumbest ideas you ever had. Look where they got you. I tried to warn you."

Hitler could laugh at this, and at other references, right up to when Bertie said, "...and, Herr Adolph, why did you insist on persecuting the Jews? You knew that was wrong."

At this, Adolph turned into a raving maniac as he tried to strangle Bertie in front of everyone. But Craig, Nicholas and other members of our staff were ready for this, and they soon had Adolph, once again, in a position of restraint, and were directing him toward the Quiet Room.

"Why did you lead Adolph on?" I asked Bertie afterward. "You knew when you mentioned the Jews that he was likely to go into a rage."

"Because," Bertie said in a slight whisper, "I needed to break through to his unguarded natural *persona* to find out whether or not he was real, or just some clever actor. And I can tell you this: he's real, all right! I heard that same laugh and saw that same fury, back in 1938, when I visited him before the Second World War. The facial expressions, the inflections of his voice, even the way his body tightened on the right side as he became angry—all these were exactly like the man I once met. Now come here, Patrick, I have something to ask you."

He motioned me toward the patio, and we went outside to a far corner near some rose bushes. "Patrick," he said, "I have an idea. I want you to join me in testing each and every one of these so-called celebrities, to see whether or not they are real. I'm proposing that you and I do some simple computer research, and then test these people on little things like the names of relatives, schools they went to, things they wrote or were reported to have said, and so on."

"Well then, Mr. Wells," I said with a big smile, "let me start with you. Since I have read more than thirty of your books, I am more than a little acquainted with many of your characters and ideas. Let me test your own veracity."

"Fire away," he replied.

"All right then, there is a character in one of your novels who was a gentleman of culture, who was shipwrecked on an island, and who saw no humans other than savages for several years. He then escaped in a strange manner, fought in World War I, and returned to this island. What was his name?"

"Mr. Blettsworthy, of Rampole Island," Wells replied, "which is also the name of the novel. I wish we could discuss Mr. Blettsworthy's wanderings at length, but I fear that in our present project, time is of the essence. So let's get on with more questioning."

"All right, then, in your *Outline of History*, what do you have to say about *Pithecanthropus Erectus*?"

"This is the so-called walking ape man," he answered. "The top of his skull, some teeth, and a thigh bone, were found in Java near Trinil. This species is believed to date back to the Early Pleistocene Era, or First Ice Age, some 500,000 years ago. But much more important than this species was the later find of *Sinanthropus*, or Peking Man, which was considered, in those days, to be the missing link between ancestral apes and today's human race."

"All right, fair enough," I said, "Now one more. What were you best known for as a student at the Midhurst Grammar School?"

Wells smiled and replied, "I was known for sitting in the back row and making flatulent noises during boring lectures, causing great laughter in the classroom. Fortunately, I was able to make these noises without changing the expression on my face, so that nobody could prove it was me. Here, let me give you an example."

The sound of an enormous fart thundered throughout the patio and into the common room, while Wells' face betrayed no motion whatever.

After one of the biggest belly laughs I had issued in years, I replied, "Bertie, that's fantastic! I can't believe that any impostor could have done it better."

"Very well," he replied. "Then let's get back to work. Why don't I take those closest to my era: Eleanor Roosevelt, Thomas Jefferson, Ludwig Beethoven and Michelangelo. And you can take Buddha, Jesus and Joan. Let's not bother testing Adolph. I'm convinced that he's all too real."

And so it went, for three long days; looking up questions on Google, and comparing the answers with those given by our residents. All of Bertie's subjects passed his tests with no problem. However, two of my subjects proved to be difficult. Since there were no accounts of the lives of Buddha or Jesus written while they were alive, I had to use the very sketchy writings of the *New Testament* and other such chronicles. Nevertheless, I told Bertie at the end of our study, that I was convinced that both Jesus and Buddha exemplified the teachings for which they were known. And the miracles which both of them had performed before my very eyes put them in a special demigod category.

*****

For some reason, Bertie chose Thanksgiving as the best time to reveal our findings to the larger group. The Rosewood Common Room was decorated with a large oil painting by Mike of the Mayflower pilgrims, their neighboring Indians, and the feast they shared. A sonata called *Gratitude* had been composed by Ludwig, and he played it beautifully before dinner, on the harpsichord contributed by Jesus. The natural fantasy of all these historical figures together was enhanced by the soft candlelight, and I must say that the Rosewood staff prepared a most delicious array of meats, vegetables, fruits, desserts and wines. And at the end of the table, at the insistence of Eleanor, was an empty chair and setting, placed there in the event of an arrival of a surprise guest before the end of the evening.

All the residents were together at the table this time, and there were toasts and jokes and increasing laughter as the wine took effect and a sense of camaraderie took over the group as never before. I was sitting at a separate table with Craig, Tawny and Nicholas, as Bertie got up to deliver his speech.

"My friends," he began, "it is the highest honor of both of my lives, to be in such distinguished company, and to speak to you on matters of great concern to everyone here."

"In my simple life in England," he said, "I endeavored to understand as much as I could about the human species and its place in time and space. And toward the end of that first life, around 1946, I found myself tormented by the thought that mankind, with its advanced weaponry and pig-headed brain, hadn't a clue as to how to survive for very long. But that was then."

He paused.

"And this is now. Each of us now finds ourselves reborn in some fashion, and sitting at this table, wondering so many things. First and foremost, *are we real?* Are we truly the same people we were—celebrities from history, with memories and skills brought all the way into this twenty-first century? And my answer to that question is, *yes*, we are real! In the modest study which Patrick and I have just completed, there is no way that any of you could know so much about your character, behave so much like your character, and look so much like your character, as to be mere actors, or people with coincidental delusions. And to tell you the truth, I myself feel exactly like my namesake, Herbert George Wells. No, every one of us is quite real!"

He paused again.

"So now I move on to another question: *What is going on here?* There are twelve beds in this curious Rosewood environment, and so far nine of them have been filled. Out of the nine, there are seven men and two women. Eight are from the Western side of our civilization, and only one is what we might call Eastern. There is somewhat of a mix in terms of what we are known for. We have three artists: Mike, Ludwig and myself; two religious figures: Jesus and Sid; and four strongly involved in the politics of their day: Adolph, Joan, Tom, and Eleanor. I would venture to guess that, assuming that this pattern continues, our future company might include people such as Abraham, Aristotle, Asoka, Cleopatra, Darwin, Marx, Mohammed, Napoleon, Newton, Nietzsche or Gandhi. But of course since we have only room for three more in our hallowed institution, the possibilities are limited."

"I would suggest Moses!" Jesus cried out from the far side of the table.

"And I Charlie Chaplin!" Eleanor exclaimed. "We could all use more laughter."

"And I, the great composer, Richard Wagner!" yelled Adolph, who was definitely feeling part of the group now.

"Yes, indeed," Wells replied. "There are certainly many good candidates. But let me move back now to the larger question of *what might be happening here.* Now I don't, for a moment, believe that the driving force for our presence here is mental health. We may all have mental or emotional challenges, but we do not fit into the normal mental health patterns. To begin with, we have all been brought back, as it were, from the dead. That is not normal. Second, we are all icons of our respective fields, and a gathering of such unusual people is not normal. And third, none of us have any interest in following the modern treatments that are meant for people with our supposed diagnoses. Some of us may need them, but none of us want to take them at this time. No, to put it simply, in this Rosewood setting, we are rebels resisting the heavy hand of modern psychiatry."

As I heard this last statement, I glanced at our director, Nicholas, who might have been troubled by that last remark. But no, with his ever-open mind, he was smiling at Bertie and clearly enjoying the speech.

At that moment, a troop of five of Glacier County's highest-placed managers strode into the room with purposeful looks that had nothing to do with Thanksgiving. The leader, a man called Stonewall, declared, "I have it upon good authority that the nine of you are presently engaged in some kind of conspiracy against Glacier County, in which you are determined to resist our medicines, our rules, and our efforts to treat your illnesses."

"Therefore," the second manager added, in an apparently well-rehearsed statement, "we have decided to disperse you to other treatment centers around the State of California, where you will no longer be able to feed on each others' antisocial ideas."

"This decision," chirped the third manager, "is to take effect immediately. So, all residents, please put down your spoons and forks, return to your rooms, and gather your possessions. The transport vehicles are waiting outside."

The shock was so strong that none of the group said anything for a moment. We just sat there in silence. I, of course, thought of the likelihood of my immediate job loss. And then I thought of Jesus, the miracle worker, who had stood up to other county managers in similar previous situations. I glanced at him, but he was just sitting there, dumbfounded.

No, this time it was Buddha who rose to the occasion. "Fellow beings," he said to the fearsome five, "you may not be aware of this, but there is something occurring here at Rosewood which is far beyond your limited brains to comprehend, and over which you have no authority."

"Grab him!" the fourth manager yelled to Nicholas and the rest of us staff. "Restrain this man at once, and take him to the

County Jail. We shall not put up with such impudence!"

The fifth manager, smaller of stature than the rest but anxious to be counted among his almost-peers, exclaimed, "This is exactly why we are here tonight—to impose law and order on a rebellious community which needs to be taught a lesson!"

The tone of all five men was firm, and clearly they meant what they said. However, the message was somewhat diluted when, with a nod of his head, Buddha turned them into chickens. For a while, the five manager/chickens tried to assert their authority through a kind of high-pitched clucking. The desired effect of shock and awe was not achieved, and so they went scurrying out the door of the Rosewood office on their little webbed chicken feet, into the building's main hall. Once there, they ran as fast as they could, with much nervous clucking, past other curious workers, and out of the building.

Meanwhile, Nicholas was no fool. After seeing, once again, the powers of certain members of our group, he was not about to try to challenge them with an assertion of his own authority. Instead, he said, "Mr. Wells, please continue."

Unfortunately, much as the rest of us wanted to hear more of Bertie's speech, before Wells could stand up again, there was another interruption.

"Ladies und gentlemen," came a resonant voice from the direction of the Rosewood office, "Beggink your forgiveness for beink so late to dis party, I vish permission to join you."

It was a surprised Nicholas who (despite having no advance notice of the coming of this stranger), greeted the man, welcomed him, and asked that he take the empty chair at the end of the table.

"And will you please tell us your name?" Nicholas asked in a gentle voice.

There was no need for any of us staff to have this question asked. For looking at him, his big doe eyes, his bushy black moustache, and his long, unruly white hair, we already knew.

"Mein name," said the stranger, "isht Albert Einshtein."

CHAPTER THIRTEEN

Al E.

Sex is such an elusive thing. It starts with the brain and works its way down to lips, fingers, breasts, genitals, and other body parts mashing against each other in a most ridiculous manner. It's not rational. That part of the brain is unwelcome. And its emotional side has an enormous range— love, hate, envy, grief, power, revenge—anything but indifference. It demands the full attention of the spirit and body. Even when inactive, it lurks in the shadows as a force to be reckoned with.

Sex at Rosewood was also elusive. No one talked about it in the patio or the Common Room, and yet it was there somewhere in the minds and behaviors of all of its residents. As an amateur anthropologist, I tried to discern what was happening behind the scenes. Most of the residents were male, and two of them—Mike and Ludwig—had retained the kind of virile masculinity that was so attractive to the opposite sex. For them, Rosewood was like a candy shop of young, nubile night-workers who were more than ready to lay down their bodies for both pleasure and service.

Tom and Eleanor were connected—both of them with aristocratic backgrounds and endless ideas on the nature of humankind, and I suspected that their constant delight in the affairs of the mind crossed over to the physical side of life.

In a moment of surprising candor, Jesus admitted to me one day that his relationship with Mary Magdalene had been more than platonic, and that he now wondered who, among the Earth's numerous residents, might be his offspring. I suggested, perhaps rudely, that his affair had occurred so long ago that maybe all of us today were his children. Even me! He laughed at this and suggested that we keep this little secret to ourselves.

Sid, on the other hand, was a sexual enigma. According to history, He had lived a normal marital life and even had a son, Rahula, before leaving his palace in Lumbini. The Four Noble Truths which he later espoused rejected all desire, but were generally not interpreted to exclude sexual desire. Had sexual desire been eliminated, or even reduced, this would have had an enormous effect on all life. It appears that Buddha felt fine about almost all of mankind's worldly pleasures: sex, good food, games, etc. It was only when deprivation of these caused suffering that he injected his theory about detachment. Here at Rosewood, I watched him carefully to see if he evidenced any signs of pleasure about such things as the food or pretty women. For the most part, he appeared to be indifferent to any kind of pleasure or pain. But there was one time when I saw his eyes light up more brightly than usual. It came after one of our female social workers kissed him, fully and unexpectedly, on the lips.

I've saved the worst for last. Yesterday I saw Joan and Adolph holding hands as they walked together down the hall toward Adolph's room. I was tempted to wait a few seconds, and then knock on Adolph's door to admonish both of them for breaking one of Rosewood's strict rules. But I didn't.

How on Earth could Joan be so stupid, so misguided, so crazy as to even think about relating to Adolph like this? He was such an old, disgusting, vile, twisted, deranged creature; and she was so pure, so innocent, and so deserving of a good, decent man! Then again, I thought about Joan's need for a militant cause, and about how Adolph's perverse mission to conquer the world could be the answer to that need. At that moment, I wrote Joan off as nothing more than another crazy patient in my facility.

*****

There were several loose ends left over from our Thanksgiving dinner. For one, I was quite disappointed that Bertie never finished his speech. He told me later that the two distractions—the turning of county managers into chickens, and the arrival of Einstein—had upset his focus to the point where he had no wish to continue. He further said that he wanted to speak with Einstein "to run by him a few ideas about time and space."

Buddha's passing remark that the Glacier County managers "had no authority here" intrigued me. If so, who did? Was Buddha himself controlling events? When I asked him this question, he smiled and shook his head enigmatically. "No, Patrick, there is something else outside of us all which is unfolding, and I have no clue as to what it is."

Another loose end was a comment that Jesus had made to me several weeks ago. He had said, within minutes of his arrival, that he had been looking forward to meeting me here. When I eventually asked him about this, he said, "Patrick, I just knew that there would be someone here at Rosewood who would be our, shall I say, guide. You're the only staff member who has seriously studied history, and who has a passionate interest in other cultures. You're the only non-resident who is asking questions about where mankind is going, and the truth is that you belong in this group every bit as much as Einstein, Buddha and me. You're not an outsider looking in. You're one of us."

"Such flattery," I replied, "will get you everywhere. But I don't believe you for a second. I'm nowhere near the same level as any of the rest of you."

"You're not well known," he answered, "but that doesn't matter. What does matter is that you have qualities which can bring all the residents together as we prepare for what lies ahead."

"And what does lie ahead?" I queried.

"I don't know," he said with a smile. And that was the end of that perplexing conversation.

This brief encounter spun my head around, for it made it look as if I was close to the center of this craziness. Was my mind inside some kind of narcissistic dream? It was absurd enough for me to be spending time with Jesus, Buddha, Jefferson, and the like, but for Jesus to be calling me "one of us?" How insane! The only thing that made sense was that I was somehow part of a Grand Delusion! And that Hitler might well be the only one here who had made sense, when he exclaimed early on that everyone around us was just an actor carefully trained to drive us crazy, for God-only-knows what purpose.

Meanwhile Mike was progressing well on his circular painting of the Roseville residents on the ceiling and walls of our Common Room. He had completed the first nine residents, and was now starting on our latest member, Albert Einstein. All his portraits were exquisite, done in the heavy life-like style of four-teenth-century masters, with rich oil colors, soft skin tones, and expressive eyes. Soon there would be only two more to go.

Out on the patio, his large sculpture was literally shrouded in mystery. Mike had it covered by a thick canvas, and heavy ropes with intricate knots made it difficult for anyone to untie. When he wasn't painting our Common Room ceiling, he was work-ing day and night by flashlight under the canvas. He absolutely refused to talk about this sculpture, much less let anyone catch a glimpse of it. More and more, he was sleeping outside in the patio beside his treasure, like a yard dog.

*****

Our latest resident, Al E., had not come to us through any of the normal channels. There was no strange behavior in the community, no 5150 by police, and no screening by the Sutter Roseville Hospital. He had no record with any of the county departments. As far as we could see, he was an ordinary citizen, and had no business at all being at our facility. A polite "good-bye and good luck" would have been the most appropriate treatment of this new character on the scene. However, he fit in so well with the other "dead celebrities" that Nicholas made no effort to turn him away. In normal times, Al would not have lasted five minutes at Rosewood. But these were not normal times.

The next morning, as I sat across from Al in my small Rose-wood office, I looked closely at his large black eyes, his long nose, and big, bushy moustache. "Sir," I began, with the defer-ential title I felt was due, "I need to ask you about your life. To begin with, where were you born?"

"I vas born in ze town of Ulm, in ze year 1879. Mein fader Hermann vas an engineer, und mein mudder raised ze family. Ve ver Jewish, as you may know, but not shtrict Jews. Ve seldom vent to synagogue."

"What would you like to tell me about your work?"

"Vell, I belief dat mein discovery of ze Special und General

Theories of Relativity are vell-known. Most of zat verk vas done in Berne while I vas a full-time patent officer for ze Sviss goverment. Mit no staff, no laboratory, no assistants und hardly any assistance from uder scientists. Vell, maybe a little from mein wife Milena. Oh, if I had only had more help during zat time, tink of vat I might haf done!

"Anyvay," he continued, "vat I found zer, und later at ze University of Berlin, in ze fields of photon theory, und quantum theory, und in ze relationship of time to shpace und light und matter, forever changed ze way ve look at ze verld!" Al stopped here. It was like everything to follow needed to come from a different channel. He looked away from me, and then at me, and, at last, whispered in a trembling tone, "Do you vant more?"

I said yes, and awaited Part Two.

"Do you vant to know vat is ze matter?" he said, in worried, rising tones. "Everyting! Everyting! First I see from your computers zat ze cosmological constant is positive! Do you know vat zat means?"

I shook my head.

"It means zat ze universe ist not shtatic, but expanding! Und zen I find zat ze speed of light may not be constant! Do you know vat zat means?"

I shook my head.

"It means zat all mein theories of relativity are kaput! Kaput! Kaput!"

He paused and went on. "Und zen I find myself here mit people like Jesus und Michelangelo—und you! In ze twenty-first century! Do you know vat zat means?"

I shook my head.

"It means zat ve are all living in some kind of crazy parallel universe, having passed, perhaps, through a shtupid vorm hole, und zat time und shpace are no longer meaninkful! No longer meaninkful, mein friend. and do you know vat zat means?"

I shook my head.

"It means zat you und me und eferybody else here are illusions! Illusions! Zat ist all ve are!"

I was silent.

He was walking toward the patio.

"Yavold, mein friends!" He was now talking to anyone who happened to be around. "All of mein theories must be trown out ze vindow! As garbage! Garbage! Garbage! So vat am I now? A dumkopf! How you say it in English?"

"A nincompoop," Wells contributed.

"Yah, un nin-com-poop! I...am...a...nincompoop! Nincompoop! Nincompoop!" he shouted as he crossed into the patio.

The last thing I wanted was for Al to have a heart attack and die for the second time during this interview with me. I asked him to calm down, but this was unsuccessful. Instead he proceeded toward the rosebush and yelled out, "Dumkopf! Dumkopf! Dumkopf!" And then again, "Nin-com-poop!" before moving into a German which I could not understand.

What happened next was a spectacle which I shall never forget, partly because so many of our residents became involved, in different ways, and partly because there was so much shouting, seemingly all at once. Unfortunately, almost all of it was in German, so I had to make do with asking Tom Jefferson to translate the different rantings for me, after it was over.

It all began with my interviewee, Al, screaming something about how his whole life had been a failure, and punctuating this statement with the grabbing of a large clay pot filled with a withered tomato plant, and slamming it down on the cement into a thousand pieces.

Then Mike, standing guard over his precious shrouded sculpture, yelled to Al in German, "If you take one step closer, or if you break one more pot, I'll kill you!"

At that moment, Adolf ran into the patio and screamed in the high-pitched Nazi voice which I'd heard before so many times in movies, "Albert Einstein, you are a traitor to ze state! Heinrich, take zis man avay immediately!" (I guess Adolph's mind had regressed back into an early-1940s Germany, when SS Chief Heinrich Himmler might have been at his side.) The rest of Adolph's speech was filled with ugly swear words, interrupted by five people who were shouting almost as loudly.

Joan appeared, swore eternal allegiance to der Fuehrer, and stated that she was willing to take on all enemies for the good of the state. But der Fuehrer told her that she was only a girl, and that she needed to stay home and have Aryan babies. She became furious at this and yelled that such stupidity was the reason that Hitler lost the war. If he had let German women fight and work in factories, this would have doubled the size of his force and he would never have lost! To this, he replied that no one could talk that way to *der Fuehrer* and get away with it, to which she replied that she just did!

Meanwhile, Al had not stopped screaming, and this time it was aimed at Adolph, whom he accused of genocide, to which Adolph replied, "Shtupid Jew! Ve never should haf allowed you und your family to eshcape! Ve should haf sent you to ze ovens of Auschwitz!" At this point, several other people screamed something on this subject back at Adolph.

Then Eleanor made an appearance, and, ever the peacemaker, she tried to persuade these "grown men" to "take a deep breath and calm down." But Adolph had particularly vile words to say about her and her husband Franklin, whom Al then defended, all in a shouting mode.

As I looked around the patio, I noticed that Buddha and Jesus were sitting together on a bench, watching the show with no apparent interest in participating or interfering. Buddha had a glowing smile, and Jesus a brow wrinkled with disgust. Bertie was sitting at a table, laughing uproariously, and every so often making caustic remarks to his new friend, Ludwig.

It wasn't long before our Rosewood leader, Nicholas, entered the scene, and strode heroically to the center of the shouting. I followed him dutifully, as did several other staff members. "Gentlemen!" he announced. But Adolf and Al continued their shouting so that no one there could really hear. Nicholas and Scott put Adolph in a restraint hold and dragged him off, still screaming, to the Quiet Room.

It was my gut feeling that things were getting out of hand

at Rosewood. A short time later, I went into the office of our Director and said, "Nicholas, I'm thinking that, for the good of everyone, both residents and staff, it might be good to hold off temporarily on the admission of more patients. We need a period in which to settle down."

But just as he replied, "That sounds like a good idea, Patrick," his phone rang announcing that Scott had accepted another resident. The fax came five minutes later.

*****

PATIENT: *Abraham Lincoln (aka Abe Lincoln, Honest Abe)*

RECENT HISTORY: *Patient was found sitting in a snow-storm in front of an Auburn War Memorial to U.S. soldiers who had given their lives for their country in recent wars. He said he was deeply depressed about the state of the nation, and had been for a long time. He mentioned no financial or other support from friends or relatives, and he appeared to be disoriented in terms of who he was and why he was here. He was placed on a 5150 hold for grave disability and taken to the Sutter-Roseville Hospital. After being medically cleared, he was transferred to the Roseville Psychiatric Facility.*

BACKGROUND: *Patient claims to have been born on February 12, 1811, in a one-room log cabin in Hardin County, Kentucky. He lost his mother at age nine, he resented his father's lack of education, and his family lost their land several times due to major debt and legal problems. After jobs as a storekeeper, Illinois militia captain, and postmaster, he began to practice law in Illinois in 1837. He said that he was successful mainly due to his storytelling, and that this also helped get him elected to the U.S. Congress in 1846. He spoke out against slavery (with a plan to return them to Africa), and also against the "unnecessary" 1846 war with Mexico.*

Patient claims he was elected President of the United States in 1860, and that he served during most of the 1861-65 Civil War period. During this time, he admits being depressed "every single day" due to the loss of fellow countrymen, the death of his son Willie, and a carriage accident which deepened the depression and irrational behavior of his wife, Mary. At the time of his assassination by John Wilkes Booth in 1865, he felt that he had largely failed as a President, even though the Union was being preserved.

MEDICAL HISTORY: *Major brain damage from a bullet wound to the head; hereditary cancer syndrome (multiple endocrine neoplasma, type 2B); evidence of past syphilis and malaria*

PSYCHIATRIC DIAGNOSIS: *Severe depression, bipolar, post traumatic stress disorder*

*****

The staff had grown accustomed to the admission of dead celebrities, but this one seemed particularly challenging. Abraham Lincoln's somber face on pennies and five-dollar bills, and his gaunt figure in the nation's capital, had come to epitomize deep depression, much of it due to the bad luck of being President during the worst period in American history.

One question which was on my mind concerned the facial appearance of "Honest Abe." If, by some miracle, he, too, was being brought back from the dead, would he bear a hideous scar from the bullet wound inflicted on him by John Wilkes Booth on that night of the assassination in Ford's Theater? I had read that the wound had entered near his left ear, and had exited near his right eye. How could this possibly be fixed to make him look like the Lincoln we would recognize? Another of the many mysteries remaining to be solved.

CHAPTER FOURTEEN

It

It all started around 4:30 p.m., when I was conducting my last check of the Rosewood premises, before heading home.

Two soft, slender arms pulled me into the darkness of one of the rooms, and down onto the nearest bed. Candles were the only light, and incense filled the air. The body pushing me down was clothed in silk, and the grip was hard, insistent. I tried to say something, but two luscious lips closed in on mine before I could utter a single word.

I struggled a little, but not enough to free myself from this sudden bondage. I didn't know what to do. It had been a long time since I had felt the curve of a woman pressed against me, and there was a strong inclination to just let things happen. Yes, I was violating the rules; but no, the door was closed and we probably wouldn't be caught. And yes, it felt wonderful!

I let out my breath, relaxed, and allowed two hands to run their delicate fingers behind my head, and onto my shoulders. I was getting excited. Very excited. I didn't want this to stop, but didn't encourage it either. No, I just lay there, and let fate take its course. *Just a little more,* I thought, *and then I would end this craziness.*

But no, I didn't end it. My mind couldn't keep up with the racing pleasure. It deserted me, and I became lost in a whirl of uncontrollable desire.

I grabbed Joan's arms and held her down below me at the foot of the bed. I forced her mouth open and kissed her brutally, with anger, rage! And she yielded, and sent the same brutality back to me, as we devoured each other. Two animals engaged in mutual murder, and suicide!

I was going to violate her, so help me God, and *nothing could stop me*... until my hands felt the touch of something hard and cold, something metallic, something so sinister that I couldn't imagine how it got there!

Yes, believe it or not, there it was! Fastened securely through the ages, protecting this virgin warrior, was a chastity belt! A crude device constructed to allow her to perform the necessities, but prohibiting any hungry male from entering the poor sweet thing's little chamber.

I stopped. The excitement disappeared, and Joan began to cry.

I held her in my arms, kissed her softly on the forehead, and contemplated the predicament. My God! This poor thing had been living with the crude device forever, and no one in this century had noticed! Wasn't that strange? Don't doctors do complete physicals anymore? My thoughts went to Adolph, and I felt relief that at least he had not penetrated this little thing, either.

And then, ever the problem-solver, I pondered how to get this thing off of her. I certainly couldn't report it myself. Questions would be asked. And I wasn't sure that Joan wanted to come right out and ask for it to be removed. Somebody might ask her why. So I came up with another plan. I would tell the night doctor that Joan had reported a rash on her leg. That would do it.

Then I went home.

CHAPTER FIFTEEN

Abe L.

At 3:28 p.m. the next day, a man of unmistakable countenance walked through the front door of Rosewood, followed by a young male social worker and a middle-aged nurse. He was quite tall, maybe 6' 5", and dressed in black from head to toe. He wore an 8-inch stovepipe hat that made him look even taller, a dark suit and pants, a black bow tie, and a white shirt, all from the 19th century. His face was angular, and it bore the wisdom of a man who had suffered over a long period of time. But there was also a sparkle in his eyes that led one to believe that beneath the grave exterior was a sense of humor. A slight scar near his right eye was located where I suspected a fateful bullet had exited, and a black, salty beard and bushy eyebrows completed the picture.

"My name is Abe Lincoln," he told us softly, with no expectation that we might have heard the name before. "Pleased to meet you folks." He shook the hand of everyone in the room like a seasoned politician.

Nicholas smiled broadly as he said, "The pleasure is ours, Mr. Lincoln. We hope you enjoy your stay here." Nicholas proceeded to tell Abe about the rules of Rosewood, and I gave Mr. Lincoln a tour of our modest facility.

After introducing Abe to his new roommate, Tom Jefferson, I sat down with him to ask a few questions. I started with, "Have you ever been to a place like this?"

"Nope," he answered. "It's a might bigger than the log cabin I grew up in, and a might smaller than the house I was living in when I was inconvenienced."

"Inconvenienced?" I replied. "What do you mean?"

"Oh, it's a long story...about men fightin' and women cryin' and a whole country gone to Hell. I don't reckon we have time to go into that right now. Besides, I could use some sleep."

Respecting his wishes, I walked him back to his bedroom, where Tom was waiting with an excited look on his face.

Two hours later, I heard the two of them still talking in their room, and figured that Abe was not likely to get much sleep that night. When dinner was announced, they strolled into the

Common Room, looking like the best of friends, and I took the liberty of saying, "If you don't mind, can I ask what were you two were talking about in there?"

"Oh not much," Tom replied. "It just seems that we have a slight disagreement as to the nature of liberty."

"Yes," said Abe. "Tom here thinks that we should have let the South go their own way before the Civil War, and that it wasn't important to preserve the union."

"That's right. It would have saved the lives of hundreds of thousands of citizens, and the grief of a whole lot more."

"But at what expense? Have you no pride in the country which you yourself helped to produce, and which holds dear the greatest principles known to humankind?'

"The greatest principle I helped write was in the Declaration of Independence: that one people should have the right to secede from the larger government when the differences are strong enough. Did you ever read that document, my friend?"

Abe's brow grew tense as he answered this jab in a less than civil tone. "Tom, anyone who has read my Gettysburg Address knows that I hold your Declaration in high regard. I have also read that you thought our government should be destroyed every generation through the 'blood of tyrants.' Is this true?"

I could see that this argument was going nowhere, when into the room walked a diminutive man with beady eyes and a cold stare.

"Who's he?" Abe asked.

"Well," I said good-naturedly, "Let me introduce you." I beckoned the man to come over and said, "Adolph, this is Abe Lincoln. And Abe, this is Adolph Hitler."

Abe stretched out his long bony right arm to shake Adolph's hand, and said in a gentlemanly fashion, "Adolph, nice to meet you." But Adolph was in no mood for pleasantries. Rather than hold out his hand, Adolph sent a large wad of spit onto Abe's outstretched right hand. And faster than a sledge hammer bearing down on a wedge to split a rail, Abe's right hand smashed into Adolph's chin and sent poor Adolph sprawling back five

121

feet onto the Common Room floor.

"No man's going to spit at me like that and get away with it," said Abe. "I've had enough of this gnarly creature." He walked back to his room.

Adolph did not reply. He was out cold, and it wasn't until Scott and I took him back to his room that he opened his eyes and began nursing the bruise on his jaw.

*****

After dinner, I took a stroll down the residential corridor of Rosewood and pondered the almost perfect placement of room-mates. There was Jefferson and Lincoln, as just mentioned, both passionate builders of the American nation, with infinite ideas about the nature of man and our political institutions. There was Beethoven and Michelangelo, both moody artists whose genius transcended the human limitations of their respective art forms. There was Jesus and Buddha, two immense spirits of the universe. Joan of Arc and Eleanor Roosevelt were like two sisters of different ages going through life together: one a naive child looking for strength and reassurance, and the other a fortress of wisdom and compassion, looking for a cause to mother. Then there was Albert Einstein and H.G. Wells, the foremost scientist of our time matched with the brilliant and prolific futurist, both searching for the meaning of life in the cosmos.

There was one more space to be filled at Rosewood, and that person would inevitably be paired with Adolph—the misfit, the miscreant, the despised symbol of all evil. Adolph, the one who didn't fit in with anyone, but without whom, somehow, our world, our civilization, would not be complete. I racked my brain trying to think of whom this last resident might be, and the possibilities I came up with included Rasputin (but he wasn't large enough in history), Caligula (he, too, felt like a comparatively minor celebrity, stuck in his old Roman era), and Osama Bin Laden (but he had died recently, and this would have broken the pattern). No, there was no one to compare with *der Fuehrer*, and worthy of being his roommate. Even the great historian/social thinker/futurist H.G. Wells was at a loss to predict whom the twelfth and final resident in our facility might be.

*****

It was midnight on the eve of December 20th when we got a call, and later a fax, from the Sutter Roseville Hospital, directing us to take a new patient to fill our last vacant bed.

PATIENT: *William Shakespeare (AKA Edward de Vere, the Earl of Oxford, Francis Bacon, and Christopher Marlowe)*

RECENT HISTORY: *Patient was found on the second floor of the Roseville library at 2:30 a.m., reading a book of Elizabethan-period sonnets by candlelight. He was a man of about 60 years of age, 6 feet in height, 200 pounds, black eyes, and a receding grey hairline. He was dressed in blue jeans and a black turtleneck shirt, with a well-worn leather jacket. He had with him a large suitcase from ancient times, in which there were many changes of 16th and 17th century clothes, some of them worn by noblemen and others by peasants of the day.*

When confronted by police, he drew a sword and threatened to run it through anyone who came close. Eventually he was stun-gunned into submission, and 5150ed as a danger to others. He was taken to the Sutter Roseville Hospital, cleared in a medical check-up, and transferred to the Rosewood Psychiatric Facility.

BACKGROUND: *When asked his name and background, patient was evasive. He began by claiming that he was William Shakespeare, the famous 16th century playwright and poet. Then he claimed that no, he was really Edward de Vere, pretending to be Shakespeare. Then he claimed that no, he was really Christopher Marlowe, pretending to be Edward de Vere. And finally he claimed to be the Earl of Oxford, pretending to be*

Christopher Marlowe. He further stated that he was an actor who could play any part he wished "on this strange, new stage," and that the world would never know his true identity. "For all intents and purposes," he added, "I might even be the Lord High Commissioner, Sir Francis Bacon!"

When asked for more details about his life, patient stated that he had lived during the English reigns of Queen Elizabeth and King James, and that he had written many plays and acted many roles in the theater of that time.

MEDICAL HISTORY: *Patient was found to be suffering from two forms of cancer: the first evident in the tear duct in his left eye (Mikulicz's disease), and the second, a protuberance in the nasal corner. Otherwise he appeared to be in good health for a man in his sixties.*

PSYCHIATRIC DIAGNOSIS: *Schizophrenia, delusions of grandeur, delirium due to infective psychosis, paranoid personality disorder*

*****

Once again, the staff mused about our imminent meeting with perhaps one of the greatest personages of our civilization. I had seen around ten of Shakespeare's plays (my favorites being *Hamlet, Macbeth* and *Twelfth Night*), and had committed to memory one of his sonnets:

When, in disgrace with fortune and men's eyes,
  I all alone beweep my outcast state,
    And trouble deaf heaven with my bootless cries,
    And look upon myself, and curse my fate.
Wishing me like to one more rich in hope,
  Featured like him, like him with friends possessed,
    Desiring this man's art, and that man's scope
    With what I most enjoy, contented least,

And yet, with all these thoughts, myself almost despising,
  Happily, I think on Thee, and then,
    Like to the break of day arising from sullen earth,
    Sings hymns at Heaven's gate,
For thy sweet love remembered, such wealth brings,
That then I scorn to change my state with kings.

Ah yes, it was time now to meet the famous bard.

CHAPTER SIXTEEN

At the Mall

At 9:03 a.m. on December 21, Jesus was reported missing from the facility. Rosewood is a small place, and it didn't take long to discover that he was not in his bedroom, the Common Room, the TV room, the patio, or any of the bathrooms. He had not communicated anything to anyone, so we had to follow protocol.

At 9:22 am, we called the Roseville Police Department to report a missing resident. He was not technically on a 5150 hold, but since he had not told anyone that he was leaving, we needed to report him anyway, as a concern. When we told them his name was Jesus Christ, they laughed at first, and then said, "Yeah, we've heard that one before." Then we described him as around 6 feet tall, 160 lbs., dark-skinned, black scraggly hair, wearing a plain black tee shirt, jeans and sandals, with a gold ring in his left ear and a string of common stones round his neck. He was not physically violent, but he was passionate about many areas of life.

There was considerable speculation between our Rosewood staff and the Roseville Police about where Jesus might have gone. Since he had originally been found near a camp for homeless people, it was thought that he might be there, or at Glacier County's only homeless shelter. But no, there was no trace of him at either place.

*****

It wasn't until 4:35 that afternoon that we got a call from the Glacier County Sheriff's office, informing us that Jesus was alive and more or less well, and that he would be returned by squad car to our facility in less than an hour. The story of what had happened came out in bits and pieces, and most of these accounts made no sense at all. The only comprehensive description was found in an unpublished article which my friend, Fred Smedley, of the *Roseville Independent News*, sent to me the next day.

Jesus Meets Santa at the Galleria
by Fred Smedley

For the most part, I consider myself to be a reasonable human being. I have two arms, two legs, and two eyes to look at the life I see around me. For fifteen years, I have been writing articles for this journal, and, interesting as I try to make these stories, I can't think of anything exceptional which I have written—nothing truly extraordinary, until now. Yesterday I was assigned to cover the story of the day—Christmas shopping at the Galleria Mall, which, as everyone knows, is an important subject at this time of year, but also so predictable that it's hard to make exciting to readers.

Yes, there were a lot of people at this mall yesterday, and a lot of worried faces, as though failing to find the perfect present for Cousin Vinnie would result in a lifetime of guilt and unforgiveness. Luckily, I had my good cell phone with me, and so I got that priceless shot of a woman dropping a mountain of beautifully wrapped packages, and another of a young boy trying to carry something that was clearly too big for him to wrap his arms around. He just sat on the floor and bawled his head off while his father screamed at him to "Stop crying and be a man!"

It was approximately 2:15 p.m., near the piano player on the First Floor of Nordstrom's Department Store, when I got my scoop of the day. I saw a young man, about six feet tall, in a while robe, heavy beard and thong sandals, racing through the store. Just as I pointed my camera at him, he stopped at a counter where wool shirts were on sale for $79. He grabbed three shirts out of a man's arm and threw them up into the air, while shouting for all to hear, "Is this how you celebrate my birthday?"

129

He crossed an aisle, slammed his fist through a glass jewelry case, and picked up a beautiful diamond necklace. "Is this what I'm all about? Diamonds, gold, and rubies?"

He crossed over to the beauty section, where the most expensive scents in the store were being sniffed by ladies in elegant furs. He picked up several bottles and smashed them to the floor, saying, "I hope no one in here is a Christian, because if you are, your souls are destined for the fires of Hell!"

At this point, salespeople were calling Security, and all shoppers within earshot were staring at this man with the beard.

"Sinners!" the man yelled as he jumped onto the piano in front of me, "It's not too late to head the calling of the Lord! I urge each and every one of you to put down your purchases, leave this mall, and go out and make this a better world!"

Now I'm no expert on the Bible, but I can certainly remember the scene in the New Testament where Jesus had a temper tantrum in the Jewish temple, and where he overturned their tables and scattered their coins. This man's use of the word "I" meant that he really thought that he was Jesus. Actually, he did look a little like the Jesus depicted in paintings, who had lived two thousand years ago, albeit a little darker-skinned. And his words had a certain truth in them.

At a shoe counter, he grabbed a pair of alligator boots on sale for $199, and he tossed them as far as he could across the store. "Is this your idea of Christmas?" he yelled. "How stupid! How ignorant! Have you never read the New Testament? Have you never heard that it is harder for a camel to go through the eye of a needle than it is for a rich man to enter the Kingdom of Heaven? Have you never heard, in the Old Testament, the story of the golden cow? Fools! How dare you commit such *sacrilege in my name? Idiots! Idiots!!"*

Several security guards had arrived, and were trying to clear Nordstrom's first floor shopping area of all customers. But most of the people were reluctant to leave, as they were curious to hear what this strange young man had to say. "Jesus!" rang out a voice emanating from a large man in a blue suit, who looked like a store manager, "Jesus, let me talk to you!"

The man who called himself Jesus turned to face the creature in the blue suit and said, "What do you have to say?"

"What I have to say is this," the store manager replied, lowering his tone in an attempt to calm Jesus down. "Since you lived, more than two thousand years ago, things have changed. Americans have found that the best life for all is a combination of your Christianity and what we call Capitalism. We have married your concept of love with our concept of desire. We provide for ourselves and for the poor by hard work, and by shopping. This store is what you might call a Modern Temple, in which everyone's desires can be satisfied by making lots of money, and then spending it. This, in turn, helps other people satisfy their desires, and brings jobs and prosperity to our nation. Christianity and Capitalism is a marriage made in Heaven, in which everyone thrives through a common pursuit of pleasure. We have come a long way since your days in the Jewish temple with the moneychangers!"

Jesus looked at the man with a gaze that indicated that he was struggling to understand this totally foreign type of thinking.

"What's more," the blue-suited man added, "When you break things like that jewelry case, you reduce yourself to the level of a common criminal. This property does not belong to you, and you have no right to damage it. So please, do not do any more damage, and I pledge here

and now that you will not be charged with any crime."

"No!" came the reply. "No, no, no! I cannot accept this! I know there are people nearby with no food or shelter, and your pursuit of pleasure is an excuse for rich people to stay rich at the expense of the poor. You are a false prophet, and I will continue to spread the true word of God."

With this, Jesus ran off to another area of the mall. I followed him, in pursuit of my scoop of the week.

I don't think that "Jesus" had any idea what stores were located where in this mall. His next stop, seemingly chosen at random, was a video game shop where several teenagers were shooting at each other in the latest version of the game, Grand Theft Auto. They were laughing at all the blood in this particular version as Jesus approached, looked on, and wrinkled his brow in disbelief.

"This is the work of the devil!" he yelled at them. "This game is all violence! How can you enjoy this?" As he yelled this, Eminem's "Love the Way You Lie" began to play in the background.

"We ain't hurtin' nobody!" the older boy replied. "It's just a game. And who are you?"

"My name is Jesus," came the reply.

"Jesus? Hey Dude, you look like Jesus!" the taller one responded. "And I like your outfit. Where'd you get those sandals? And those beads, and the ring! Wow!"

"Hey, Buddy," said the other boy, pointing his cell phone at the bearded man. "I'm gonna put you on YouTube and make you famous! What d'ya think of that?"

Jesus seemed a little confused. He had apparently come here to preach about the sins of modern culture, and was being made into some kind of celebrity, based not on what he was saying, but on what he was wearing.

"Boys," he said, "Do your parents know you're here?"

"Yes, sir," the smaller one replied. "They drop us

off here any chance they get. They say it keeps us out of trouble."

Jesus didn't linger in that shop any longer. He acted like he had more important things to do. Meanwhile, three security guards were watching him from a short distance. At that moment, he wasn't making a disturbance, so they didn't confront him, but they felt a need to follow him, just in case.

Jesus passed a bright yellow Lamborghini, parked on a red carpet in the middle of a corridor, and he jumped on top of it. "Good people!" he yelled. "This is not the way to Heaven! If you have enough money to buy these things, spend it on helping the poor. We have people, even children, with nothing to eat, and no shelter. You need to share your wealth with them, not squander it on yourselves or others who are rich. If you have one drop of Christian blood in you, heed my warning and share your riches with others. Otherwise, you will be damned to the fires of Hell. Nothing less! Did you ever hear the story of the man who had two sheep, and he gave one away. He wanted to slaughter the other to feed his family, but..."

Jesus was drawing a crowd.

The security guards were now accompanied by regular policeman, who were pulling out their stun guns. "Sir," one of them called out. "Come down now, or we will be forced to shoot!"

"In whose name are you acting thus?" Jesus replied. "If it is in the name of Rome, or America, or some other government, then leave me alone. I have no quarrel with you at this time."

"You're disturbing the peace!" replied a police Captain with more patches than the rest of them. "You're in violation of Roseville Mall Ordinance B86775, Section 201, Subsection C. Come down immediately and give yourself up, or we'll shoot!"

"Ignorant fools!" Jesus said, "Anyway I don't rec-ognize any of your authorities as my *authority, and I have work to do."*

With this, he leaped off of the Lamborghini and onto the floor like a stuntman, and raced through the gath-ering crowd toward the center of the mall, followed by around ten policemen and security guards, many of them with stun guns drawn. I, of course, ran after them in pur-suit of my scoop of the month.

At the center of the Galleria Mall is a large open space which, in this season, is reserved for Santa Claus and the long lines of children waiting patiently to see him. When Jesus arrived at this scene, he was moving so fast that his momentum propelled him through two lines of children and one line of parents, and directly onto the lap of a very fat, smiling Santa Claus, who greeted him with a jolly, "And you, young man, what would you like for Christmas?"

Jesus, sprawled awkwardly in Santa's lap, looked up at this apparition, and just stared at him for a few seconds.

Santa continued in what he thought was the true spirit of the season. "Well, young man, I hope you've been good this year, because if you have, Santa has some great presents to bring to your home on the night before Christmas. Ho Ho Ho..."

By this time, the crowd at the center of the mall—children, parents, shoppers, and policemen alike—had stopped doing whatever they'd been doing, and were fo-cused on the spectacle in front of them; the black-beard-ed white-robed figure sitting on the white-bearded, red-suited Santa's lap.

"What's your name?" Jesus asked the man in red and white, innocently.

"They call me Santa Claus," the man replied, finally realizing that this stranger was clueless as to who he

was. *"My job is to make presents for children who have been good, and to bring these presents to their homes every year to celebrate the birth of Jesus. And what, may I ask, is your name?"*

"My name is Jesus," the bearded figure replied. "And my job is to tell rich people not to waste money on themselves, when there is so much poverty in the world."

The two bearded men stared at each other for a moment, and then Santa reached out his right hand and said, "Pleased to meet you, Jesus!"

Jesus shook Santa's hand perfunctorily, and then stood up to address the now large crowd which had gathered. "Citizens!" he barked in the voice of a preacher. "Good citizens!"

Even the policemen were silent now, as they, too, were curious to hear what Jesus had to say.

"I have no doubt that you mean well! Buying and giving presents to each other in celebration of my birthday. I suppose this has something to do with the three wise men who reportedly visited my parents on this occasion long ago, and who gave them gold, myrrh and frankincense."

After a short pause, Jesus continued. "Mr. Claus," He bellowed for all to hear, "I have a request." (another pause) "From now on, in celebration of my birthday, instead of promising that children will receive gifts, I would like you to tell them to give to others who are in need."

Santa was silent. He had no idea what to make of this creature which had landed on his lap, and he wasn't about to engage him in more conversation. He whispered to the nearby store manager, "I think I'll take a break."

Jesus continued, speaking to the gathering multitude. "Good citizens, did you ever hear the story of the donkey who refused to go up the hill?"

At this, the police started to move in. The Captain

yelled through a bull horn, "Jesus, or whatever your name is, it's time for you to come with us!" The other officers all had their stun guns out and were pointing them at the curious, dark-skinned figure.

As Jesus began to speak again, a precocious child of about ten asked him, "Are you really the son of God?"

The answer was short and familiar, "I am what I am."

That's in the Bible!" the young boy shouted. "He must be Jesus!""

As the police came closer to Jesus, stun guns pointed at him from all directions, and the children began to shout in horror, "Let Jesus go! Let Jesus go!!"

But it was too late. Several stun guns went off, Jesus' eyes glazed over, and he slumped back on to Santa's lap. Widespread screaming commenced and many of the children began to bawl like babies. (Indeed, some of them were babies). Some of the older ones, who weren't crying, yelled things like "Murderers! You killed him! You killed Jesus!"

This refrain grew louder as three of the officers unceremoniously dumped Jesus' unconscious body onto a waiting gurney and wheeled him out of sight.

Looking around the large mezzanine, it was my guess that most of the parents knew that Jesus was not actually dead, and they saw him as some kind of nut. But the children, many of whom had studied Jesus' life in their Sunday schools, saw him as the real Jesus, the one who had been tortured and murdered on the cross. And now they were witnessing a second murder, not by Romans, but this time by their own Roseville Police! Santa was nowhere to be seen as these poor little children were carried out of the mall in the arms of their parents, crying their little heads off, as the parents tried to assure them that everything was going to be all right.

In a note to me at the end of this piece, Fred added this:

Patrick, it took me all night to write this story. As I mentioned before, I'm not used to this kind of thing, Most of what I write is fairly ordinary, but this event opened up my mind and my heart to something else. I don't really know what happened out there, this afternoon, at the Galleria. But somehow, I feel like a different person from having been a witness.

Patrick, in some ways, the follow-up to this story was as intriguing as the event itself. My editor told me that the story would never be published either on the internet or in the newspaper, because the owners of the Galleria didn't want the bad publicity. And since they had immense political power, no media or social outlet was allowed to reveal what had happened.

When I called Glacier County offices to inquire about the whereabouts of "Jesus," there was a blanket denial of any such incident having taken place. When I tried to interview the Santa Claus of that day, I couldn't find him. Another Santa Claus had taken his place at the Galleria, and the former one had been reassigned to an undisclosed location. So as far as the larger world was concerned, this event never occurred.

I wondered about all the children who had witnessed this scene, and how they might process it over time. I also wondered about how some of the adults might have felt watching this. And I wondered what was going to happen to the man who called himself Jesus.

In total frustration, I tried to think of what to do with this story I had written. I have no close family members to share it with. (My three ex-wives ran off long ago.) I don't really have any close friends. But then again, I do have one old buddy who might relate to it, a guy who works for the Rosewood Psychiatric Facility. You!

CHAPTER SEVENTEEN

Bill S.

It was 1:45 in the afternoon when the man who sometimes called himself William Shakespeare strolled by himself through our Rosewood door, leaped onto one of our desks in full green kilt and a patch over one eye, curtsied, and delivered this brief soliloquy:

> *Gracious members of the Rosewood staff,*
> *I entreat you to discern, now, wheat from chaff,*
> *For standing before you on this occasion*
> *Is the famous bard from Stratford-on-Avon.*
> *And, like it or not, you shall all be treated*
> *To some foolishness, while you are seated.*
> *For Hamlet, Falstaff, and the witches' feared toad*
> *Are now in the wings of this humble abode.*

This short speech, though hardly reminiscent of Shakespeare's great works, was delivered with such eloquence that there was nothing left for the six of us staff members in attendance to do but applaud. And applaud we did, all on our feet, yelling, "Bravo! Encore!"

The figure standing above us, in green-checkered kilt, brown vest, and full grey beard, smiled down at us with the confidence of one who's totally comfortable with his trade.

"Friends, Rosewoodians, Planet Earthians," he continued, and then in a softer voice, "I haven't the slightest clue who you are, but you appear to understand the King's English, so I welcome you to my new stage."

Nicholas stepped forward and said, "And we, Mr. Shakespeare, welcome you to our modest facility. We hope that you will find your stay here to be as enjoyable as it is useful." With this, he introduced each member of the staff, and asked me to give our new guest a tour of the facility.

As the green-kilted bard walked into the Common Room, he asked me how many residents there were here.

"Twelve," I replied, "yourself included."

"Splendid!" he answered. "That's perfect."

"Perfect for what?" I inquired.

"For a play," he answered. "You don't expect me to sit here in this room just twiddling my thumbs."

"No." (I wondered whether this expression went all the way back to the sixteenth century. For all I knew, he had invented it.

Introducing Bill to the other residents was a little awkward at first. Shakespeare appeared to have heard of only three of the residents: Jesus, Buddha, and Joan of Arc (who had all lived before his time). And of course, none of them had heard of him. The others, who had lived after his time and knew his name well, greeted him with great interest, and he found this a bit confusing. "I know that a few in the London circles of my time were acquainted with my work," he told me, "but I am confounded by this larger fame."

As I introduced Bill to the other residents, I noticed that he was treating these introductions as auditions. He asked each "player" (as he called them) if they had ever done any acting, and, if so, what roles. He asked about their passions; what made them mad, what made them laugh, and what made them want to dance. He did this in so joyful a manner as to cause some of them to lose all inhibition. He did a kind of jig with Mike, Tom, and Eleanor; and everybody laughed, until more residents joined in—even me! He made Joan well up with tears as she talked about the burn marks on parts of her body, and he induced Ludwig to issue forth a tirade against the "autocratic snakes" who had been his patrons. With Adolph, he opened up the channels of racism and allowed him to speak out against Jews, Communists, and people of color. When other residents began to protest, he calmly motioned for them to relax and allow this "exquisite force of nature" to "speak his peace."

"Yes!" Bill said at last, after each resident had been interviewed. "Each of you will have an important role! And what a splendid cast we have! Never, even in the days of the old Globe Theater, has there been so much talent to work with! Praise be to God, the king, the players, the audiences, the pit trash, the devil, and the asp of the mighty queen of the Nile, for this moment in time! I hereby declare to all of you that I am now, at this moment, profoundly happy!"

*****

Bill's ebullience was infectious. As the Christmas holiday approached, most of Rosewood's residents were hard at work preparing for the occasion. Mike was busy finishing his sculpture, which was due to be unveiled on Christmas Day. Ludwig was working on a symphony, also to be debuted on that day. Others were working with Bill on their parts in the play. And, as has already been mentioned, the occasion bore a special excitement since we would actually be celebrating Jesus' birthday with the man himself!

There were discussions about whether presents would be appropriate, and if so, what Jesus would want. There was talk about whether toasts would be fitting at the end of the dinner; and, if so, who might say what about whom. Someone brought up the fact that Jesus had had twelve guests at his table at his Last Supper in Jerusalem, and Eleanor chimed in with, "But of course! To make it twelve this time, we'll put an empty chair at the table!"

Under Nicholas' direction, Rosewood had always celebrated Christmas day with a feast, and had also honored the birthday of each resident. So having a double celebration of Christmas with Jesus' birthday was the natural thing to do.

I told Brigit that night that on Christmas day I would break the rules and invite her over to meet Jesus, Joan, and all the other people I had been telling her about. I had nothing to lose, and she was thrilled!

CHAPTER EIGHTEEN

Darkness

As night follows day, as cold weather follows warm, and as death follows life for all living forms, the residents of Rosewood went from euphoria to depression in just a few hours.

The central figure in this was Jesus, the man who was about to be honored on his birthday, but who was in no mood for such a celebration. His experience at the mall had left him distraught, and was made worse by his watching the news of the day on television: Muslims fighting a mostly Christian army in Afghanistan, Jews fighting Muslims around Israel, drug dealers fighting governments in Colombia and Mexico, and poor people struggling to survive in places like Sudan and Somalia. On the night before Christmas, he insisted on controlling the remote, and every so often he switched from the news to other shows like American Idol, CSI, the Gem Network, and a show comparing mansions for sale in Monaco.

Toward the end of his eve, he declared to everyone in the Common Room that he wanted to call the whole thing off. These were his words; "Kind friends—and I do mean that, for I have come to love each and every one of you—my first life has been a total failure, and therefore I feel that there is nothing to celebrate.

"I have tried to preach service and poverty, yet my birthday is celebrated as an orgy of rich people buying wasteful presents for other rich people, while the poor are left to fend for themselves. I have tried to preach peace and tolerance, yet so-called Christian politicians still have their soldiers fighting others thousands of miles away.

"I have tried to preach obedience, yet this planet's Christians continue to defile my teachings in my name. And here we are, gathering to celebrate my birth and my life as if nothing were wrong! No! I won't stand for it! I have lived in vain, and I won't be a part of such hypocrisy, such shame, such evil!"

We were stunned. Yesterday we had felt so happy to be preparing for a glorious day of sharing. And today, it was all falling apart.

In the midst of this crisis, Buddha lent another perspective.

"Fellow beings," he said, in his soft, wizened way, "may I say something?"

Jesus looked at this other holy man, lowered his voice to a more humble tone, and replied, "Yes, of course."

"May I suggest," said Sid, "another kind of celebration. Why not make tomorrow an honoring of the love we feel for each other here and now in Rosewood? Let's overlook the planetary conflicts for one day, and just live in the moment."

This simple speech was persuasive. We looked at Jesus as he pondered this idea. Then he said, "Yes, Siddhartha, you are right. It's not for me to burden you all with my troubles. Let the celebration be held, and I will try to work through my challenges in my own way."

With these words, there was no cheer in the room. No sudden change back to the manic joy of yesterday. No, just one thing was said, for all to hear. A simple acknowledgment, by the Buddha: "Thank you, Jesus."

*****

Buddha's words and Jesus' reluctant acquiescence to hold the party did not stop the "night before Christmas" from being one of the worst that Rosewood has ever endured.

Later that day, Bill (Shakespeare) came to me, eyes welled up with tears. "Patrick," he said, "there's no way that I can present this play tomorrow. When I came here, it seemed like a good idea, but I hadn't really thought it through."

Like a good social worker, I gave him my full attention.

"First," he said, "I don't have enough time. Just a few days! To write a whole play! With twelve characters! I'd be hard-pressed to do this in a month, or even a year! And then the different languages! How can you possibly have characters talking to each other if they don't speak the same language? Or have an audience which speaks only English understand somebody speaking German or Italian? And then the different cultures! Good Lord, I come from sixteenth-century England. How can I

145

understand someone like Siddhartha who's from the fifth century B.C., much less a twentieth-century Eleanor Roosevelt? I'm lost! Lost in time and space! It just can't be done!"

None other than Adolph came to the rescue. With Jefferson translating, Adolph said, in a pleading tone, "Bill, you *musht* present zis play. It's perhaps mein only chance to tell ze world ze second part of *Mein Kampf*. I have been defiled for decades, and I insist on telling the world my side of mein shtory. Even if you don't produce any other part of zis play—und even if I haf to write every single line meinself—I *must* do mein scene. I *inshist*!"

Upon hearing these words from a diminutive man who had inflicted and felt more suffering than perhaps anyone in history, and who certainly had a good story to tell, Bill shook his head and said, "Patrick, I have no idea how this is all going to turn out, but I can see now that, at least as far as Adolph is concerned, the show must go on."

After this came a flood of other Rosewood residents who were having doubts about the party tomorrow, about the play, and about their lives.

Eleanor, the one who was known for being cheery and keeping a stiff upper lip, complained about Bill's pressure to get everyone involved. "He's being a bully," she said plainly. "Not everyone enjoys getting up and speaking in front of people, and he's tormenting others to suit himself. It's not fair!"

"Yes," Joan agreed. "I'm a warrior, not an actress. I want no part of zis play."

Tom added, in a squeaky voice, "As you may know, the reason that I never delivered my State of the Union addresses to Congress in person is that I'm not a good speaker. Nor would I ever be a good actor. I can write, and that's about it."

"So what are you saying?" replied Bill. "That we should call the whole thing off except for Adolph? Great! No play! Fine! I now have just one last request for this group of illiterates: get me back to my own time, where the theater was appreciated, and indeed revered. I have no use for any of you!" He stomped out onto the patio and slammed the glass door behind him. Fortunately the glass didn't break.

Through the glass door which was slammed but didn't break, I could see Mike throwing down his sculpting tools with disgust. "I can't do it!" I heard him yell. When I went out to ask him what had happened, he replied, "I just broke the nose! The God-Damned nose just broke off! Here I've been working for weeks on this face, and there's no way I can do it without the nose! I may as well destroy the whole piece! It's no good to anybody now!"

He picked up a sledge hammer and was about to smash his precious artwork to smithereens when I stepped between him and the canvas-covered sculpture.

"Mike," I said softly, "please don't do this. Whatever you have done, I'm sure, is valuable to some people. I'd like you to stop thinking about your work for a few minutes. Just calm down. Maybe there'll be some way to fix it."

Mike had always been good-natured with me, even during moments of tempest. After looking at me with moist eyes, he said in Italian, "Bene, Patricio," and returned to his room.

Then there was Ludwig. Poor Ludwig, deaf to the world, and struggling to produce another great symphony with almost no tools to work with. He wrote down these words in German, which Tom translated dutifully. *My mind is filled with the dark sounds of an opera I once wrote, and I can't escape these sounds to finish my work for tomorrow. I'm so sorry.*

I looked into Ludwig's eyes with some kind of understanding and told Tom to translate: Ludwig, my friend, just do the best you can. Here are just a few details on the problems which other residents told to me on that day. Abe was obsessing over Tom's idea that the Civil War had not been necessary, and that he was personally responsible for the deaths of a half million Americans. Bertie was upset that our jubilant Christmas celebration was turning into a nightmare, and by everybody else's being upset. The Rosewood staff was upset that we had just received word that the facility was about to be shut down, with its residents shipped off to unknown locations and its staff laid off. The memo cited some legal concept called Termination at Will and ended with the blunt statement, "All staff must have their desks emptied and their keys turned in by 9 a.m. on December 26." There was no apology, no contingency plan, no thought of help for us workers and our families. Nothing. But then that was the way of Glacier County upper management for as long as I could remember.

CHAPTER NINETEEN

Embers

Later, around midnight, there was a spontaneous gathering of residents in the patio. Someone built a fire, and residents brought out chairs, sat around the embers, and talked.

It was not like a midnight mass, as some residents had been accustomed to attending at this hour in their past life-times. For one thing, Jesus was not there, and it would have been awkward to hold one without him in attendance. For another, they felt a need to come together, to rekindle bonds while facing the prospects of separation and uncertainty.

"You know what I'd like to do when I get out of here?" said Abe. "I'd like to go with Tom on a trip to visit some of the places where we used to live. Yes, I'd like to see Monticello, and then go back to the White House and take a tour, and see my bedroom again. And then walk across to the monuments I hear they've constructed in our memory, and go back to Gettysburg and again pay my respects to the dead. I'd like to show Tom the old log cabin in Little Pigeon Creek, where I grew up, and the courthouse in Springfield, where I started my campaign for President. What do you think, Tom?"

"With you at my side," replied Jefferson, "I could do it. Otherwise it would be too sad. I'd like to visit the home of my dear friend, John Adams. One of my greatest regrets is that I didn't take the time to go up and visit him in person while I could, especially in those later years."

"Abe," said Eleanor, "it was at your monument in the capital, that I had one of my most treasured moments—listening to Marion Anderson sing on the steps before a crowd of 75,000 and a radio audience of millions. But I have no desire to go back to the White House."

"Where would you go?" asked Tom.

"Oh, maybe China, India, France, and Brazil, to get some idea what's happening in the rest of the world. You can take my body out of Planet Earth for a while, but you can never take the United Nations out of my old body."

"Eleanor," said Joan softly. "Wherever you go, I'd like to go too. You have been my tower of strength, and I couldn't bear to lose you as a friend."

"That will never happen, my love," replied Eleanor. "And where would you like to go?"

Joan thought for a while and then answered, "To be honest, I feel a need to fight one last battle—somewhere, anywhere! For the glory of God! Then I'd like to get married to a nice man and settle down and raise a family." This spun my head around. I would never have thought this of her. And it opened up further speculation.

There was silence, and Tom spoke up again. "How about you, Mike?"

Mike spoke in Italian, and Tom offered this translation. "Oh, me? I might be doing exactly what I'm doing now—painting, sculpting, creating works of art for the glory of God. Only this time it would be different. The world has changed, so I'd look into some new art forms, maybe holographic movies."

"And you?" Tom wrote down for Ludwig. Ludwig wrote something back, which Tom translated for us: "Ludwig wants you all to know that he feels very comfortable here. He likes this group of friends and would like to remain with you for as long as possible. But he says that if he had to go somewhere else, he would like to return to Vienna and write music there for the court, or for whoever the current rulers are."

"And you, Al?"

"Shtrange as it may seem," Einstein said, "ze first ting I vould like to do would be see mein own brain. As you may know, before I died, I asked it to be preserved und shtudied. Und it vas. Most of mein brain vas kept at a laboratory in Princeton, close to ver I worked, and I vould like to compare it to ze brain I haf now. After zat, I vould like to take a tour of ze CERN accelerator in Shvitzerland. I haf a million—no, two million qvestions for zes people."

Sid was the next one asked to speak, and his statement was as brief as most of his others. "As you know," he said, "I don't care about these things. All life is perfect, wherever I happen, or not happen, to be."

Bertie was the last to speak.

"Like Ludvig," he said, "I find you all to be quite pleasant company. I am content to venture into whatever lies ahead. I feel like I'm back in the time machine of my first novel, and, for the present, am enjoying every minute of it."

As for the others, Bill and Adolph were in their respective rooms, preparing for the day ahead. And Jesus was in his, suffering with his own special anxiety.

*****

It happened again that night, or more accurately, early the next morning—my first Christmas present of the year.

As I was making my final rounds, two soft arms pulled me again into Joan's room, and onto the nearest bed, with candles blazing and incense smoldering. This time I offered no resistance at all.

CHAPTER TWENTY

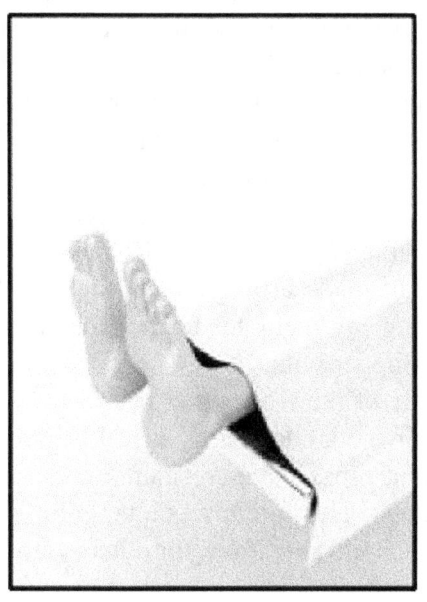

Guests

Most of the Roseville residents slept late on Christmas day. There was no eagerness to look for presents, as is the custom in most American and European families. Indeed, for most of our adult cast of characters, there was nothing but dread about what might happen on this day, and in the days to come.

The notable exceptions were Adolph and Sid, an unlikely pairing. Adolph was itching to tell his story at last, unencumbered by fear (for Rosewood was perhaps the safest place on Earth for a man like him to speak freely). And Buddha was Buddha, with an impenetrable sense of calm and joy, in spite of the many other moods around him.

My thoughts were with my daughter, whose destiny was about to plummet into a world of uncertainty. Our nice home, our free-roaming German Shepherd doggies, our planned vacation to Colorado, food for our next meals—everything was in jeopardy as I pondered what my jobless next stage might bring. But at least I had made arrangements for my old friend, Fred Smedley, to bring my daughter to the Rosewood building and share this Last Supper with us.

In the middle of the Rosewood party chaos, I was charged with logistics for food, chairs and such. I began with a table for thirteen: Jesus, the other eleven residents, and an empty chair for the unknown guest. Then there was a table for twelve staff, and some additional chairs and tables for others who might find their way to this miserable affair.

"Patrick," I heard Tom say, "may I suggest that you arrange the chairs on one side of the tables, with everyone seated on the outside, so that we might see each other with an unencumbered view?"

I said, "Sure, Tom." What I was really thinking was *What the Hell do I care? As of tomorrow I won't be working for this lousy outfit, anyway.*

"Say, Patrick?" came Bill's voice from another direction. "We shall need a larger space than this Rosewood Common Room."

I agreed to hold the event in the cafeteria, which was much larger, and in the same building but outside of our Rosewood facility. I decided not to tell anyone in upper management about this. *Why the Hell should they know, and what the Hell did I care?*

For the food, I figured that I'd start by asking Jesus, the birthday boy, for requests. He responded with a grimace that suggested that he might not even bother to show up. When I asked the other residents for ideas, Tom recommended the food which Jesus had enjoyed on our outing: kosher lamb, potatoes, and lentil soup. I thought this was fine, and decided to supplement it with some salad and vegetables, and one of my favorites, a cherry cobbler dessert. I figured that we couldn't go wrong with bread and wine. And the wine might loosen everyone up a little.

Then there were the decorations. A traditional Christmas tree with lights, ornaments, and presents seemed a bit much for the Jesus we knew, but we did bring in two small fir trees on stands, and put them behind the main table. On a small table between them, Nicholas set up a crèche scene of a half-manger made of wood, with little figures of Joseph, Mary, Baby Jesus, three wise men on camels, a lamb, a donkey and some sheep. Behind the manger was a red light to give the scene a soft glow. This was all that we figured Jesus might tolerate on his birthday.

The party was scheduled to begin at 2 p.m. By 11 a.m. the tables, chairs, and food were under control. Scott, Tawny, Craig, Nicholas, I and other staff wore prim black and white serving outfits.

I'd slept little the night before. My head was buzzing with everything from losing my home and job, to losing my connection to Jesus, Jefferson and the other luminaries in my life. This event was feeling more like a wake than a celebration. As usual, in moods like this, my stomach became nauseous, and I doubted that I would able to hold down any of the food which had been prepared.

Toward noon, I fell asleep on a chair in one of the far corners of the cafeteria. The last words I remember hearing inside my brain were from an old Shakespeare play, "Sleep, that knits up the ravell'd sleave of care..."

*****

At 1:30 p.m. the first two guests arrived for the party. They were my precious daughter Brigit, looking beguiling in a red and white velvet dress, escorted by Fred Smedley in a button-down white shirt and khakis specially pressed for the occasion. I led them to a table in the back of the room.

The next guests were a total surprise; seventy-two members of the Auburn Symphony Orchestra, dressed in formal black-and-white attire, and carrying their respective instruments. The bass player, a jovial man called Steve, whom I happened to know, said with a big smile, "Patrick, I have no idea why we're here, but it looks interesting." Without really thinking, I welcomed them and seated them in the back part of the room. I was glad that I'd heeded Bill's request to move the event to the larger venue.

The next guest was a corpse. Yes, the corpse of a young man whose body had apparently been burned to death, and which was carried in on a gurney, wrapped in a white sheet, and attended by the deceased's mother and two brothers. The mother spoke in Arabic, which was translated to English by one of her two sons. "We were told that there is a man here named Jesus, who works miracles and who might be able to bring my son back from the dead. That is why we have come here today."

I had no idea how this woman and her family had heard about our Jesus, or about our party, or how they'd managed to travel here with this corpse from half way around the world. But then again, there are many parts of this story that I can't, and never will, understand.

Nicholas greeted the family with kind words, translated back to Arabic: "Ma'am, I can't guarantee you anything in relation to your son, but you and your family are welcome to join us for this

Christmas, and to share our food and our company." We helped wheel the gurney to a special side table, and found chairs for the three other family members.

*****

The next guest was a total surprise—America's youthful President, Barack Obama. He was dressed in a very black suit with an expensive red tie. He was smiling so wide that you could see every one of his perfectly polished teeth. He was preceded and followed by dark-suited Secret Service people, who proceeded to check out the other guests and staff in a no-nonsense pat-down search for weapons.

Meanwhile, the President, in the style of most politicians looking for votes, worked the room clockwise, shaking the hands of each of us in turn while saying, "Nice to meet you." He missed no one, starting with Nicholas, then me and the other staff, Brigit and Tom, the seventy-two members of the Auburn Symphony Orchestra, and the corpse's family. I think he would also have shaken hands with the corpse, had this presented an opportunity for garnering one more vote in the next election.

So awed were we that he was here, that no one bothered to ask him why. I figured it might have something to do with a mental health announcement, or perhaps the opening of a new federal facility as part of his stimulus plan. At any rate, he was seated at a table next to the gurneyed corpse.

Unfortunately, gregarious as he was, after he sat down, there was no one for our President to talk to, given the generally quiet nature of corpses. So I went over to engage his interest in some topic or other. "Mr. President," I said awkwardly, "have you some particular interest in mental health?"

"Well, as a matter of fact, yes," he replied with a grin. "There are a lot of people who think I'm crazy to have taken on this job."

I followed with, "Is there something in particular that we can do for you?"

157

"Well yes, actually, I'm here to see Mr. Lincoln. I've heard that he was in residence, and I've always wanted to meet him, even it's only a facsimile. Sorry I didn't call ahead. I happened to be in the neighborhood, and thought I'd drop by."

"Mr. President, Abe should be with us shortly. Is there anything else I can do for you on this Christmas Day?"

"Yes, as a matter of fact, my wife and daughters are waiting in a limo outside. Do you think they could come in?"

"But of course."

"And..." (Then he began to whisper, and he covered his mouth, so that no one else could see hear or see what he was saying.) "...I've heard that there's somebody here called Jesus whom I would also like to meet. Do you think you could..."

"Yes, of course," I whispered back.

Two minutes later, a stunningly beautiful and well-dressed trio of ladies—Michelle, Sasha, and Malia Obama, were escorted into the room by more dark-suited Secret Service people, and were taken to seats at the same table as the President.

The next surprise guest at our celebratory event was a small girl in a motorized wheelchair. She was mute, and in ordinary circumstances would not be worthy of much attention. She wore a modest pink dress which could have doubled as a nightgown. Her skin and hair were dark, and her legs were withered. When her tiny right hand rapped on the outside door of the cafeteria, I barely heard it. I thought it might be a rattle caused by the wind.

But when I looked down, there was a presence of some powerful energy that could not be denied. I opened the door for her and said, "Welcome."

She nodded, and drove her wheelchair over to where my daughter Brigit was sitting. Brigit was thrilled to have a girl her age at this affair, and they smiled and gave each other a big hug.

Behind this new little girl were a man and a woman dressed in Arab headdresses, robes and sandals. They, too, had an aura of belonging, so I led them to chairs next to the little girl in the wheelchair.

Following these three guests were three more: a dwarf who

introduced himself as Rich Barton and the author of a book called *Another Messiah*, a stunningly beautiful Brazilian woman who introduced herself as his wife Maria, and their son, a blonde boy called Peter. They were seated next to my daughter and the girl in the wheelchair.

*****

So there we were—around one hundred people already seated at this now major event, and as yet no Rosewood residents! It was already 1:58 p.m., and I began to panic. Had all of the residents disappeared, just as mysteriously as they had come in the first place? Were they scared? Did they think this was some kind of trap? Maybe a glimpse of some of the Secret Service agents had driven them away.

I was all set to go back to Rosewood to make sure they were still coming, when the first of our residents finally arrived. It was Sid (Buddha), who was dressed in a simple orange robe. He walked over to the far end of the main table, and sat down in silence.

"Sid," I remarked. "It's exactly two o'clock in the afternoon. I'm impressed with your punctuality."

"Time?" he answered calmly. "What is time?"

I could think of no reply, so I strolled back toward the kitchen.

The next resident to arrive was Adolph (Hitler). He was dressed in the Nazi uniform of *der Fuhrer*, with a red, white and black swastika armband, and sporting a wide, and I might add, sinister, grin. His voice boomed out a short speech in German to everyone there (which hardly anyone understood), and this was followed by a high-pitched hideous laugh that made me want to puke. He sat down alone at the other end of the main table, in the seat farthest from Sid.

Next came Tom (Jefferson) and Eleanor (Roosevelt), holding hands and giggling, as Eleanor announced, "Tom and I have just founded the Squeaky Voice Society, and we are looking for new members. Anybody interested?"

Tom added, with a grin, "Yes, and the rules are somewhat stringent. No normals need apply."

"*I'll join!*" Adolph yelled, and he let out another bloodcurdling laugh, which temporarily diminished the joyful spirits of Tom and Eleanor.

Next came Joan (of Arc), dressed in a well-tailored suit of 15th century armor. She was small, even for a woman, so that the armored figure looked more like a child. But in her eyes, which was all of her that one could see, was a determined stare. Emblazoned on the teat-protectors of each breastplate was the proud monogram, JDA.

Looking at her in full battle attire, I could not help but think of the contrast between this outfit and the silk nightgown that she'd worn during our last meeting. I wondered whether Joan was planning to fight to the death, here and now, for some cause. Glancing at the Secret Service agents, I noted that they stood ready to pounce and bring her crashing down at the slightest sign of danger. But they, like the rest of us, found her more pitiful than dangerous. She had trouble keeping her balance in all that armor. As she walked toward the head table, she almost crashed onto the floor, several times. But at last she made it.

I began to worry about how she was going to eat, since the helmet had no openings big enough through which to pass food. I was thinking that she would need a straw for water or wine. Fortunately, she had the presence of mind, before sitting next to a beaming Adolph, to take off her helmet, and reveal that pretty face.

My daughter Brigit stared at her, incredulous.

Next came a threesome of our civilization's greatest artists: Ludwig (Von Beethoven), Mike (Angelo), and Bill (Shakespeare). Each was dressed in the finest clothing of their region and time period.

Ludwig was the first to enter the room, wearing the black tails and white tie of a distinguished 18th century orchestra conductor. When he saw the seventy-two members of Auburn's Symphony Orchestra, in black and white formalwear and with all their instruments, he raised his arms high into the air, and gave a whoop reminiscent of the noise made by a cannibal called Dunu whom I had once known in the Amazon. He walked over to the musicians and shook hands with each one in turn. With huge smiles all around, his deafness was no problem.

Right behind Ludwig were Bill and Mike. Bill was dressed in an elegant dark blue and white Elizabethan-era costume, with an exquisite matching hat with a white ostrich plume, a broad coat with gold epaulettes, tight pants and matching elfin slippers. When he saw the size of the cafeteria and the potential audience of more than one hundred people, he bellowed, in a voice which literally shook the walls of the building,

Hail to Phene, for answering prayers!
And bringing space to the Rosewood players
For actions, words, thoughts, coming soon,
To this new age, shall bring a new tune!

The short speech was so beautifully delivered that most of the crowd stood up and cheered. Bill gave the audience a not-so-modest bow.

Mike was almost unnoticed, dressed in a long black robe which matched his beard, a purple coat, and short-sleeved shirt. He went right to the sidelines, where he checked the placement of the sets he had painted for the production, and also the veiled statue which was due to be uncovered later this day.

After the three great artists, came two men with some of the greatest minds in history, Al (Einstein) and Bertie (Wells). As they entered the cafeteria, they were so absorbed in a conversation about the nature of the universe that they didn't stop to notice the large crowd which had already been assembled.

"Ishn't it incredible," Al said to Bertie, "zat scientists now believe, in current Big Bang theory, zat 13 billion years ago, ze entire observable universe, shtretching out more zan 10 billion light years in all directions, vas squashed into a space much smaller zan a single electron! Und zen, in .129 fraction of von second, our universe expanded 1034 times!"

"Yes," replied Wells, "and that our universe may be just one of more than 10^{500} universes!"

When the two men, at last, looked out at the large circle of strange people in front of them, Wells said, "And what have we here?" Then they both started to laugh.

"I haf no idea, Bertie. No idea."

*****

The next-to-last resident to arrive was Abe (Lincoln), dressed in the same black suit, black bow tie, and eight-inch stovepipe hat that he wore when he arrived at Rosewood. He looked at the menagerie of residents and guests, walked over to an empty seat at the table, took his hat off, and sat down.

"Patrick," he said with a smile. "I don't think I'm in Springfield anymore."

"No Sir," I replied. "And I don't exactly know where we are either."

"You know," he continued, "the last thing I remember from my old life was that our country was engaged in a Civil War. But now I can't seem to remember exactly what it was we were fighting about. I guess my mind is not what it used to be. Could you refresh it for me?"

"Yes, Sir," I replied. "That war was mostly about slavery, and a few related matters. Do you remember issuing an Emancipation Proclamation, in which all the slaves were freed?"

"Yes, by gum, I do. It's starting to come back now."

"Sir," I said, "with your permission, there's someone I'd like you to meet."

"Yes, of course."

I walked over to the other president's table and asked Mr. Obama if he would come with me for a second. After he followed me back to the head table, I said to Abe, "President Lincoln, I'd like you to meet the current leader of the United States of America, President Barack Obama."

"Mr. President," said Obama, "it is indeed a great pleasure and honor to make your acquaintance. You have always been one of my greatest heroes."

Abe's eyes grew large as pancakes as he peered at the black-skinned man grinning at him from just inches away. The two of them shook hands heartily, and Abe said, "Glory be, I only wish that my good friend Frederick Douglas could be here with me now!"

"Yes, Sir," said the current President, "we've come a long way. But I don't think people today would be calling me 'President' if you hadn't done all you did for our people."

"Where're you from?" Abe asked.

"I was born in Hawaii, but my father was from Kenya and my mother was from Kansas. I was brought up in Indonesia, and studied in New York and Boston. My present home is in Illinois."

"Glory be! You sure do get around. Did you say Illinois?"

"Yes, Sir. I started my campaign for President at the same spot you started yours, the state capital in Springfield."

I left the two of them talking, and went over to check on the food. It was all ready, but there was concern about the warm dishes getting cold if we waited any longer for the guest of honor to appear.

Nicholas came up to me and said, "Patrick, could you check on Jesus and see if you can coax him out to join us? No pressure, no threats, just an easy request from friends."

"I'll do what I can."

CHAPTER TWENTY-ONE

In His Room

For the first time in memory, as I opened the door to the Rosewood office, the place felt deserted. Every soul who worked or resided there was at the celebration, every soul except one, Jesus. Instinctively, I knew that he would not be found in the Common Room, or the lounge, or the kitchen, or the patio. No, he would be in a much smaller place, where he could commune in peace with his god.

Of course, his room. The door was closed and all was quiet. Not a sound. At first I thought about knocking on it to give him the courtesy of preparing for my arrival. But I didn't. No, that would be too harsh, too disturbing.

As I slowly opened the door to his room, the hinges creaked, betraying my presence. At my first vision of the inside, I felt like I was entering an inner sanctum, reminiscent of my visit to the ancient catacombs of the monastery of Saint Catherine, at the base of Mount Sinai and next to the Burning Bush witnessed by Moses, long ago. There was no natural light in this room, only candles burning on the small table, the chair and the floor. The light from these candles was bringing forth shadows of the Christ on every wall, as he knelt in front of a simple alter.

He did not acknowledge me at all. He was dressed in a simple white robe, with a crown of thorns on his head, holding his hands together in prayer, and staring down at the burning candles, which in other circumstances, would have been cause for alarm and a call to the Roseville Fire Department.

I closed the door behind me, sat down on the bed, and waited patiently. For what, I knew not. For him to make some kind of gesture? I didn't know if he ever would. The celebration in the other part of the building seemed insignificant compared to this holy scene. I might wait here for hours, long past the passage of the party, and never remember that there was another important event taking place in the building. No, I was now just another stick of furniture, bearing witness to a demi-god communing with his deity. I would sit there on that bed in silence for as long as he remained in prayer.

"Patrick," he said suddenly, without turning around to look

at me. "I'm glad you're here."

I waited a few seconds and then replied, "So am I," without thinking of what that might mean.

There was more silence. I broke it with, "Jesus, is there something I can do for you?" I waited more seconds, and then added, "Would you like to talk?"

More silence. More reflection. More of my uncertainty as to what to do or say.

"Patrick," he continued at last, "can you begin to imagine what it must feel like to be crucified?"

"No," I answered. "I cannot."

"The physical pain was unbearable; but, much more important in my case, was the pain of wondering why my Lord was inflicting this upon me. And then, later, the burden of feeling like I was being tortured and murdered to save mankind. As if I, single-handedly, was responsible for the whole species which had been created in the image of God. Me! *Me! Why?*" His voice was growing in volume and intensity as he projected back to this period of sheer agony. "*Why me? Why me?*"

"But this is not the worst part of my story! The worst part by far is that I didn't save humankind from a damned thing! No, people went on killing and getting wealthy and bearing false witness and living in greed and selfishness for centuries. For millennia, after I died on the cross. And here we are today, two thousand years later, with no real change in the human condition. *Can you imagine how that makes me feel?*"

I remained silent.

"Patrick, do you know how I felt as I watched the orgy of spending at the mall. So how do I feel now? Betrayed, angry, ashamed, guilty, and depressed, just for a start! Here I am, seeing a whole human race, 2,000 years later, for the most part unaffected by my teachings. And many of my so-called Christians, are the *worst* offenders. Such hypocrisy!"

"So now," he continued, "I'm trying to figure out what to do! I've got the same ideas of peace and love as before, but I've lost faith! Yes, I've lost faith that I can do anything with this new life, after seeing what happened in the old one! Patrick, can you begin to understand?"

I nodded.

"Patrick, this birthday business is supposed to be a celebration, but I can't pretend to be happy! I'm *not!*"

Again I nodded.

"And can you understand that this 'Last Supper' brings up all those old feelings of impending doom! Of torture, uselessness, betrayal! Oh, my God, why art Thou forsaking me *again*? Are You taking me for a total fool? Are You playing with me? Are You being cruel? What's the *point*?"

"But surely there's no threat of your being crucified this time," I said softly.

"No? I have no idea what awaits me after this night is over! I have only seen glimpses of this strange new world. But I do know that rich people who call themselves Christians are, as we speak, buying wasteful presents for other rich people. In my name. And soldiers who call themselves Christian are killing other people. In my name. In the meantime, your country of America, with all of its wealth, has an underworld that sleeps in the rain and goes hungry every day. And others around the world are even poorer than that. If I were to go out there now, of course I would live with the poor, and pray with them, and try to help them. I know I would be despised by the rich, and probably killed by someone who calls himself a Christian!

"How can it be," he cried out, "that my God would send me back to Hell for a second time? And how can it be that this second life would end in anything but murder? I went through this once. Why do I need to do it a second time, or maybe a third, or a fourth, or a twentieth? When will this suffering end? And why does it always have to be me? Why not somebody else? Why not God Himself? It's *His* world! *This isn't fair!*"

"Jesus," I said again softly, thinking now of the mission which had brought me here, "I have just one request."

"What?" he said, in a defiant tone.

"I'd like to tell you a story."

"Go ahead," he replied.

"Once upon a time," I said, "there was a young man called Mohamed Bouazi. He lived in a desert town called Sidi Bouzid, not far from where you were born. At the age of fifteen, he became a simple fruit vendor to support his mother, his uncle, and five brothers and sisters. And he did it well. But every day, a government official, similar to the ones you knew in the Roman Empire, demanded that he pay them very high taxes. For ten years, he paid them.

"Then, one day, not long ago, a government tax collector not only demanded a high bribe, but also took his fruit and his scale, and slapped him in the face. When Mohamed went to the government building to ask for his fruit and scale back, he was beaten by government officials. When Mohamed walked to the City Capital to demand an audience with the Governor, he was refused.

"Then Mohamed, in front of the City Capital, poured a can of paint thinner over his head and lit a match. His body was soon burned beyond recognition, and he died two weeks later. His death has now became a symbol of protest against all cruelty in the land where you were born."

"So why are you telling me this?" asked Jesus.

"Because Mohamed's mother and two brothers have brought his dead body here, today, to this building. They have heard of your miracles, and they are asking for your help in trying to bring Mohamed back to life."

Jesus stared at the floor for several seconds. Then he said, "Take me to them."

CHAPTER TWENTY-TWO

Amazing Grace

When the door to the cafeteria opened and Jesus walked into the room, with me trailing at a respectful distance, the room grew quiet. The attention of the occupants focused immediately on him. Someone broke into song, followed by others:

> *Happy Birthday to you!*
> *Happy Birthday to you!*
> *Happy Birthday, dear Jesus...*

But the crowd soon found that the expression in his eyes was anything but joyful, that he didn't appreciate this song, and that he seemed relieved when it was ended after the third line.

After scanning the room quickly and spotting the gurney with the white-clothed corpse on it, he walked over to it and reached out to give the nearby Arab family big hugs. The mother of the corpse cried and held onto Jesus tightly, while the corpse's brothers clung to them from the side. I could see Jesus' eyes staring at the cloth-wrapped body, as though sizing up the challenge of bringing it back to life.

It was my understanding that this man had been dead for more than a year, so underneath the white cloth there was likely to be major decay, with maggots, worms and other such creatures. Should the cloth actually be unwrapped, the putrid smell of death would be unleashed on all of us in the room. I wondered how Jesus was going to do this. It was one thing to bring someone who had just died back from the dead, like God bringing Jesus back within three days. It was quite another to bring back someone whose body had decayed beyond recognition. Then again, somehow, miraculously, the twelve Rosewood residents had all been revived, after, in some cases, thousands of years. As Einstein kept reminding us, this was all a new paradigm, unfettered by the old rules.

There was no sound at all in the room as Jesus put his hands on the white cloth covering Mohamed's dead body. He was standing, looking directly at the corpse with his eyes squinted. His body started shaking, and he closed his eyes and made strange sounds which might be construed as incantations. He began to speak in what I supposed was his native tongue of Aramaic, in long, guttural sentences, undecipherable by any of us. He went on and on for what seemed like hours, but may have been only minutes. None of the crowd seemed to object or become impatient, for (with the possible exception of Sid) what he was doing was far outside of our worlds, and we were all mesmerized by his work.

Jesus' speech grew louder, and its rhythm grew faster. His eyes opened again and started glowing like balls of fire, and his body swayed back and forth from side to side. Then, suddenly, in an explosive moment, he yelled out "Praise the Lord!" and collapsed on the floor.

Soon after Jesus himself lost consciousness, there was a slight movement from underneath the sheet. Then another. And another. The folds of white cloth parted, and there appeared before us the figure of a young man. His face was ashen at first, and then took on a dark brown color. His eyes opened, and, still in shock, he looked in front of him, where his mother was standing. They embraced, long and hard. His brothers joined the embrace, and the crowd cheered. The man brought back to life evidenced no sign of decay or blood, or the smell of death, nor even the burn marks which had covered him not long ago. Nor were the sheets soiled. It was as if he had never died. I pondered the possibility that this man had never been dead, and that this was some sort of magic trick, but kept that thought to myself.

Eventually, Jesus regained consciousness and rose to a standing position. The young man's mother, tears streaming down both cheeks and ecstatic beyond belief, looked at Jesus and said something in Arabic, which was duly translated by another of her sons, "Master, you have brought my son back from the dead. Praise be to you, to your god, and to Allah!" Jesus replied (also translated by the son), "Good woman, your family has also brought me back from the dead. May you be forever blessed!" With these words, he gave each of them a hug and walked over to assume his seat at the middle of the main table.

At that moment, First Lady Michelle Obama felt moved to break out in the chorus of *Amazing Grace*. Her gospel roots took over, and we listened to her heartfelt version of this song:

> *Amazing grace , how sweet, the sound*
> *That saved, a wretch like me.*
> *I once was lost, but now, I'm found.*
> *Was blind, but now I see.*

This was followed by the 72-piece Auburn Symphony Orchestra playing a beautiful verse of the same song, and then an a capella chorus sung by everyone. The man brought back to life, Mohamed, sat down in a normal chair next to his family. Everyone else sat down, too, to enjoy our meal, at last.

*****

You know, sometimes you feel like you've got life all figured out. There comes a moment when everything is going well, when all the little pieces are falling into place and you can just sit back, relax and watch everything unfold according to plan. That's how I felt after we finished singing Amazing Grace and Jesus assumed his seat in the middle of the main table. The birthday boy was not exactly beaming with joy, but he did appear to be content enough to make us feel comfortable about being there, and I think that most everyone was looking forward to the rest of the evening.

Boy, was I wrong! The next thing that happened was a kind of sucker punch that came from nowhere.

CHAPTER TWENTY-THREE

Dragons

Before we go further, I think it would be useful to give you a brief background on two of the major forces in this story which were destined to collide.

Sasha Obama, the President's ten-year-old daughter, had a friend on Facebook who had been at the Roseville Galleria Mall on the day that Jesus had been detained. The friend, under instruction from some unknown official, had not revealed this event to any of her five hundred seventy-five Facebook friends, except for one: Sasha Obama. When Sasha received word of this event, she became fixated on the idea of her family visiting this "Jesus" on Christmas day.

When the President was told about this, he dismissed the idea as crazy, and told his daughter that they would spend Christmas at one of their homes in Washington D.C. or Chicago. That was where the rest of the nation expected the First Family to be on such a special day, and it was politically advisable, but he also told Sasha that he would have an aide "look into this Jesus character."

The aide did not find much. Glacier County's Sheriff Department and its Health and Human Services Department were quite effective in denying that they had any knowledge of a man called Jesus, or that any such untoward event had ever occurred at the Galleria Mall.

But the aide did discover, quite by accident, through a janitor he met at a donut shop, that Glacier County's Rosewood facility not only had a resident called Jesus Christ, but also one called Abraham Lincoln, who looked like the old Lincoln and even sometimes wore a stovepipe hat. When the President heard about this, he became intrigued.

It's customary for the President not to announce his travel plans too far in advance. This time, on Christmas day, he took his family, unannounced, on an unmarked plane, to Sacramento, California. When his aides tried to contact Glacier County officials about this last-minute visit, they were told that this county's managers were unavailable. The President was ready to call the whole thing off, but Sasha started crying, and telling him that this was the *only* present that she really wanted "for Christmas and the whole year!" In a moment of paternal weakness, the President relented and hastily arranged for the family to drive to the Rosewood facility. He figured that his rock-star position and infectious smile would smooth over any troubles that might arise, particularly on Christmas day. Besides, with people called Jesus Christ and Abraham Lincoln both in this facility, he, too, was curious.

*****

The Director of Glacier County Human Services was a man called Joe Thundercloud. To be truthful, Joe had no interest in service of any kind, but had risen to the top of this prestigious department through a combination of deceit and shrewdness. He never finished high school, and often told people that he was a "proud graduate of UHK" (the University of Hard Knocks).

Joe Thundercloud's original name was Howard Finklestein, and he had grown up in New York City. His mother lived on welfare, and his father was nowhere to be seen. One day, in the genealogy section of the New York City Library, he found that one of his great grandfathers might possibly have lived some-where near the Maidu Indian reservation in Auburn, California. Recognizing the potential for profit, Howard changed his name to Joe Thundercloud and forged a document attesting to his be-ing 12.5% Maidu, just enough to gain him entrance to the tribal rolls.

He brought this document with him to California in 1985, where his first stop was Alcatraz Island. This had been the site of the 1968 takeover by Dennis Banks and other Indian leaders, in defiance of the U.S. Government. Joe started claiming that he had been one of the leaders of this revolt. Though none of the actual leaders at that time had ever heard of him, this was to become a useful item on his resume.

Then on to Auburn, California, where Joe showed up at a Maidu tribal meeting, brandished his "credentials," and managed to persuade some of them that he was an authentic "Maiduian." His use of this term (which none of them had ever heard before), and his heavy Bronx accent, made them suspicious. But that suspicion vanished when he revealed a plan to build a large casino on the outskirts of Sacramento that would make them all rich. The tribal council ended up voting unanimously to accept him into the tribe, to develop the Thunder Mountain Casino in Rocklin, and to put Joe in charge of it.

His new position was short-lived. There were charges ranging from embezzlement to inappropriate behavior with female employees, which were never brought forward due to major payoffs to the respective victims. In very secret proceedings, the Glacier County Board of Supervisors decided to transfer Joe from the Thunder Mountain Casino to a post which was less likely to get him into trouble: Director of Glacier County Human Services. He agreed to this, in part, because it helped him to maintain what he called, his "squeaky-clean image."

As the Director of GCHS, Joe had two rules which were not uncommon to those in similar positions throughout Glacier County; to cut expenses and to consolidate power. In a time of fiscal concern, he received praise for moving GCHS from red ink into the most profitable department in the county. "It's easy," he told reporters modestly. "If you can make tens of millions on a casino, you should be able to make at least a few million on a service gig."

As GCHS's services moved in steady decline, he fired all employees with ideas of change, and promoted others who followed orders without question. "It's this way," he told his staff one day in a rare meeting. "You work for me, and I'll work for you. Bread gets buttered on both sides." The image may have been murky, but the message was clear: "Don't mess with me."

*****

On this Christmas day, Joe Thundercloud had been at his mini-mansion home, playing poker with friends, when the call came in from the White House. His first response was, "God Damn it, don't let them know I'm here. Tell them I'm playing golf or something." This was dutifully done. When the man answering the phone at Joe's house said, "They want to know your cell phone number, to reach you at the golf course," he replied, "Tell them I don't have it, or better yet, I forgot to charge it." With that, Joe let out a big laugh which was taken up dutifully by the others at his card table.

Later that day, Joe received word of the Rosewood party, and his first response was, "God Damn it, nobody's going to throw a party around here without telling *me*! Wait a minute! Is that Rosewood again?" He decided that "a little show of force" was in order, so he rounded up ten of Glacier County's most loyal deputy sheriffs, a group sometimes referred to as "The Goon Squad." He met them in the parking lot outside the cafeteria door, and instructed them to "just follow orders."

What Joe didn't know was that the President of the United States, with family and Secret Service, was already there. Had he known, he probably would not have shown up. There were several federal warrants for his arrest under different aliases, and he was not particularly fond of the president. In his convoluted way, he blamed this president for all the sins which past American presidents had inflicted on "his" Native American people, from Wounded Knee to Alcatraz, and everything in between. His favorite expression on this topic was, "Don't get me started!"

*****

At the time Joe arrived with his group of goons, there were three Secret Service officials guarding the door to the cafeteria. When Joe tried to walk right past them, one of them said, "Sir, you can't go in there."

"And why not?" said an already angry Joe. "I'm the Director of Glacier County Human Services. I happen to own this place. Who the Hell are you?"

"Sir," replied the officer. "We are with the nation's Secret

Service and we happen to be guarding the President of the United States."

"Ah yes," replied Joe in a sarcastic tone. "I happen to know that there are not just one, but *two* presidents in there: Thomas Jefferson and Abraham Lincoln. The problem is that they're both phony, and so are you! So I'm going in."

With that, the very surprised Secret Service agent resisted the temptation to draw his gun and shoot the party crasher on the spot. So Joe entered the cafeteria, followed by his ten sheriffs.

Joe strode to the center of the room, where he was soon flanked by his small army—and then, all sorts of things happened very fast.

"First," Joe said, loudly, "I want everyone who is not a Rosewood resident or staff member to leave the building at once. Second, there will be no party. No one asked my permission, and worse, no one invited *me*!" He took time to laugh at his own joke. "And third, whoever is responsible for this event, most likely Nicholas Leatherby and Patrick O'Leary, are hereby fired!"

"Oh no you don't!" yelled an unusually upset Nicholas, "You can't fire me! I *quit*!"

"You can't quit!" Joe yelled. *"You're already fired!"*

As this argument was breaking out, Adolph (who understood no English but intuitively knew what was going on) stood up and yelled in his fiercest German something about removing "this Jewish scum" (Joe and his policemen) to the nearest oven. At his side, Joan drew her sword and advanced toward the phalanx in the middle of the room. Unfortunately, or perhaps fortunately, she never got far. The armor was too heavy, and she ended up falling on her back and flailing like an overturned turtle until Adolph helped her back to her feet.

Other members of the head table reacted in various ways. Mike, with no weapon except for his bulging muscles, ran in front of his covered sculpture and yelled in Italian that anyone coming close to his precious art would be torn to pieces. Ludwig ran in front of his musicians and claimed something similar about protecting them. Jesus, looking exhausted from His recent miracle, muttered something about "rendering to Glacier County what is Glacier County's." And Sid just sat in his seat, watching the proceeding in a state of perfect calm, with a slight grin.

President Obama, who might have taken charge of such a situation in his role as Commander-in-Chief, was hidden from view by seven Secret Service people who stood in front in him, ready (might I say, eager) to take a bullet for the President. When several people shouted to him to take charge, he stood up on the table in front of him and announced to everyone, "Fellow Americans, (even though this didn't apply to everyone there), it's Christmas. Let's all tone down the rhetoric and put away the weapons."

"*Another impostor!*" Joe yelled. "But this one hasn't even been admitted to Rosewood yet. *Throw him out with the others!*"

I don't know who pulled the first trigger, but just after these words, shots rang out, most of them pointed toward the ceiling. Those sitting near me took refuge under the table, and I found myself face-to-face with a hatless Abe, who asked, "Is it me they're after?"

"Not this time," I replied.

On my other side, Jesus was standing tall with his arms outstretched, in a crucifixion pose. "Get down!" I yelled at him. "Please!" But no, he seemed to feel that this was another moment in which to save humankind. Farther down, underneath the table, Jefferson was mumbling something to Eleanor about the "peace and quiet of Monticello." On the other side, Al and Bertie were jokingly referring to this scene as "another Big Bang," and I heard Al whisper with a grin, "Vat do ve care! Ve're already dead!"

"Look, Patrick!" said a voice from behind me. "Watch the girl!"

It was the dwarf, Rich Barton, whose finger was pointing at the girl in the wheelchair. She was moving toward the center of the room, in disregard of the danger posed by bullets flying in all directions.

After reaching the center of the room, this little girl, who had seemed so strange ever since her arrival, said in a strong voice which rang out through the room like a thunderbolt, "*Stop!*"

Joe yelled, "*Arrest her!*"

The little girl wasted no time in using her unusual powers. With a nod of her head, she turned Joe, the Glacier County Deputy Sheriffs, and the Secret Service agents, into sheep. Yes, sheep, who looked a little like their former human *persona*, but who had to bleat rather than speak their concerns. When Scott opened the door to the outside of the building, they all ran out in a state of panic and relief.

Upon crossing the threshold of the door, they turned back into their former human selves. While Joe and the sheriffs ran off, the Secret Service agents dutifully stayed by the front door to continue their protection of the President, who waved to them from inside, indicating that he and his family were fine.

*****

Apparently, none of the bullets fired by the Sheriffs and Secret Service agents had injured anyone in the cafeteria. I will never know whether this was just plain fate, or perhaps some kind of engineering by one of our paranormal people. At any rate, after the departure of the "sheep," the mood of the room returned to normal, and Jesus himself stood up and addressed the newly formed community.

"Honored guests," he said in a relaxed voice, "I have no idea what just happened here, but I know that some people celebrate this day as my birthday, and I appreciate you all coming to enjoy this feast. And since we now have close to one hundred more people than originally expected, I shall do my best to contribute more food and wine for the occasion."

With this, he snapped his fingers and ten more fully-loaded banquet tables suddenly appeared, filled with bottles of fine wine, roast ham, turkeys, sweet potatoes, salad, fruit, and fresh-baked bread, much of it cooked to the tastes of the twenty-first century.

"Please," he added, "enjoy this meal, and this day."

With that, everyone settled down to a relatively calm meal, uninterrupted by other intrusions. Jesus spent some of that time talking to President Obama, and I spent most of it talking with the dwarf, Rich Barton, who gave me a brief description of his earlier experiences with the little girl. I was tempted to go over and introduce myself to her, but the piercing look in her eyes led me to believe that she preferred to be left alone.

For the next few minutes, I pondered my ever-deepening twilight zone. Added to Rosewood's bizarre cast of characters was now the presence of the Obama family, the Arab family, the dwarf's family, the Auburn orchestra, and this strange little girl with her retinue. I began to wonder whether there was some connection between this little girl and the return of the historical celebrities. Al had mentioned something like this earlier in the afternoon, when he said, "Zat von, Bertie, makes me dink dat she knows more zan all ze rest of us combint."

CHAPTER TWENTY-FOUR

The Trial

Toward the end of the meal, Bill walked to the center of the room, waited for silence, and announced:

What is evil, and what is not?
Our minds are cluttered in selfish thought.
The meanest man in history,
Is but a reflection of you and me.

The room went dark for thirty seconds, and then a spotlight shone on a figure standing in the middle of the room. He was short, with jet black hair and a chopped moustache, and he was dressed in a brown military uniform with a red, white and black swastika wrapped around his right arm. Adolph—our Adolph— had fire in his eyes as he spoke in German. But somehow, inexplicably, the words came out as English to the ears of us monolingual Americans. (Rich, the dwarf, explained to me later that the little girl had once arranged for a similar linguistics feat at the United Nations.)

"Damnation." Adolph stated. "Zat's me!"

"Assassin, ghoul, filth, shvine! Object of hatred by von und all! Yavold, it isht me you vant! For I haf succeeded in murdering millions—yes, *millions*—of Jews, Gentiles, Blacks, Communists, Socialists, Capitalists, und more. So many innocent people haf bin terrorized und put to death in a thousand ways. So much misery!"

He let forth the bloodcurdling laugh to which I had grown accustomed in our short life together at Rosewood.

"Am I, Adolph Hitler, responsible for so much misery? Mudders, faders, sons, daughters, uncles und aunts, close friends— all haf suffered to ze death, or been grieved for by udders. Zink of zose pictures you may haf seen at ze liberation of Auschwitz, Dachau, and Treblinka! Und *zink* of all zose who did *not* survive! Yah, it ist *me* you vant! Und it ist me zat you shall judge, here und now, in zis room, at zis simple trial."

Adolph looked at Jesus and the other ten figures from history seated at the main table. "You, mein fellow residents of

Rosevood, are mein jury of peers. Men und vimen, also from history, tried und true, to sit in mein judgment. Und I, like it or not, shall play ze role of prosecution und defense in zis trial. *Like it or not! Yavold, like it or not! For vonce more in mein tvisted life, I am in charge!*"

Nobody spoke up in opposition. After all, this was just a play. Or was it?

"I need not elaborate on mein crimes," he continued. "Each execution of mein defined ze term 'heinous!' Und zay ver repeated over und over und over, against *millions* of innocent people. Crimes, as you vould say, against humanity! Indeed, criminal codes everyver ver written precisely to protect againsht people like me. And I haf no real excuse! Or do I?"

He paused for effect here, fully enjoying his domination of the stage.

"Now zen," he went on with an enormous smile, "I ask you, vat ist evil?"

He looked directly at Jesus.

"Did not God Almighty, ze Big Man Himself, create ze Heavens und ze Earth? I zink so. It ist hritten in ze Olt Testament, in Genesis, Chapter Von. *Yavold!* You may not know zis, but I vent to a Catholic School ven I vas a young boy living in ze town of Hafeld, und I vas in ze choir, und I efen thought about becoming a priest! *Yavold—ein priest! Me!*

"So I know ze Bible teaches us zat in ze beginning, Got created ze Heavens und ze Earth, und all ze Creatures, including us, ze people—everydink in ze universe! Everydink! Everydink! Yavold! Und so He also created me! *Me!* Yah, me! So I am a creature of Got! Me! So do you vant to know who to blame for all zis evil vich I haf done? Blame Got! Yavold, blame Got! *Got!* He ist ze guilty von! Not me! I vas only following orders! *Yah, following His orders!*"

There was a long pause.

"So," he continued, "don't ask me vy I did zos terrible tings. I don't know! Zey don't make sense—not to you und not to me eder! Ask ze Big Guy! Ask Got vy He did zis. Ask Him vy He lets innocent babies die of disease, und vy He lets nice people get beaten, und raped, und killed! Ask *Him,* not *me!* I only did vat I vas created to do. I didn't know any better! *Didn't know better!"* (Another pause)

"But vait a minute!" he continued. "Got ist too far removed from zis room, and I don't think zat He is likely to come down now und answer zes qvuestions. No, I don't tink zat He can be called as a vitness. Am I right, Got? Please! *Answer me!"*

As he yelled these words, Adolph looked up at the ceiling, as if to beckon the Lord Himself to come down to this room and say a few words in this proceeding. But God never came.

"Pity," Adolph said. "But no, you are left mit me. Little olt Adolph Hitler. Poor, Got-created monster, Adolph Hitler."

Again, a short pause.

"So, ist zer any uder defense? Von might say zat I vas crazy—zat I didn't know right from wrong. But any vicious criminal can claim zis. Ze fact ist zat I *did* know zat mein behavior vas very wrong according to ze standards of most of ze vorld. Yah, of course I did! Und zes crimes ver committed over more zan tvelve years! Tvelve years! I belief zat isht called premeditated. Yah?

"Or you could blame ze German people. Zer ver around 30 million Aryans living in Germany at ze time I rose to power in 1933. I vas just von madman. By myself, I vas nothing. By meinself I couldn't haf committed more zan a handful of zes crimes before being caught und put in jail for life. So how did I succeed mit mein plan for genocide? By being followed by so many shtupid, idiot countrymen! Yah, zey belieft in vat I belieft—ze superiority of our white Germanic race! Blame *zem,* not me! *Zey* ver ze vons who carried out mein crazy plan! I vas only ze leader. Does zat make sense? Who knows? Ve vill find out.

"How about mein motif? It vas so simple: *to rule ze verld!* Und to kill anyone who stood in mein vay. It vas all qvuite rational. Ein application of Darvin's theory, 'Survival of Ze Fittest.' *I vas almost destined to rule ze planet! Und mit a few different decisions, I might haf succeeded! Yah!* Vell Okay, maybe I overdid a few of zes Jewish murders, but ze general concept vas sincere, und reasonable, und pure!

"Now zen," he continued, "you may ask, if gifen a chance, vould I do zes tings again?" Silence for a few seconds. "Yah, of course I vould! Zis ist mein essence, mein religion, or mein *dharma*, as ze Hindus vould say. I *vould do everyding over!* But mit a few modifications, of course. After all, even *I* can learn from mistakes.

"First, I vould not haf deported or kilt our finest Jewish physicists—I vould haf made zem vork doubly hard on developing ze atom bomb. Und zen I could haf bombed London, Moscow, und New York! *Yah! Ah hah!* I vouldn't haf needed our precious Panzer divisions, or our Luftwaft, or our V2 Rockets! Nein! Just a few atomic bomps vould haf done it! Und I could haf saved so many fine German lives! Zis would have been so *enjoyable!* To vatch zes countries razed to ze ground! *No survivors!*" That terrible laugh came again. "Und zen a few udder tings. I vould not haf attacked ze Soviet Union so soon. I vould haf used zat Panzer army of 4.5 million troops und 650,000 vehicles to attack *England* und its colonies. Und zen I vould haf put our fine German vomen to work, doubling production; und I vould haf listened more to Rommel, und less to Goebbels, about many tings. But all zat ist past. Let us return now to zis very moment in zis room!

"It ist time, right now, for you, mein jury of peers, to condemn me or not, as you vish. Zis is ze chance zat humankind has been vaiting for all zes years. You do vatever you feel ist right— to ze most evil man in history. I leaf mein fate in your hands."

Adolph sat down on a chair placed in the middle of the room, with a big, uncharacteristic smile on his face. He looked at the main table, where the other eleven Rosewood residents were sitting, and beamed at them. He was clearly relishing this moment. Yes, and all the attention.

At first there was more silence. Then Sid (Buddha) stood up in his orange robe to address the crowd. His tone was soft and clear, and the words (miraculously) came out in English for those of us who only spoke that language, and in German or other native languages, for the others.

"For me," he said, "there is no good or evil. I believe that everything, and everybody, just is. Therefore I cannot sit in judgment on anyone, including you, Adolph." He sat down.

"I shall take zat," replied Adolph, "as a vote of not guilty."

"You can take that however you wish," replied Buddha calmly.

"All right, zen," said der Fuehrer. "Von vote of not guilty."

Then Bertie (H. G. Wells) stood up, in a modest brown suit. "Herr Hitler," he said, "I knew you before your Holocaust. And I warned you then not to proceed with this madness. But you chose to go ahead.

"I also knew Sir Charles Darwin and his mentor, T.H. Huxley. You have distorted their concept of 'Survival of the Fittest' beyond all recognition. Their basic finding was that all species have a natural need to survive, often at the expense of others. But, Herr Hitler, the need to survive does not include sadism. It does not include the slaughtering of tens of millions of innocent men, women and children outside of your 'race' to establish a 'master race.' You are a hideous mutation of our species. So, according to all known standards of justice and decency, I must find you guilty!"

"Von guilty, und von not guilty!" Hitler shouted. He gave Bertie an icy stare before the next juror stood up to speak. It was Al, in a white shirt, gray coat and tie, and khakis.

"Herr Hitler," Albert Einstein said in pure German (but for some reason we non-German speakers could also understand him). "You haf kilt many of mein friends und relatives, und you haf terrorized mein people, und murdered more zan 6 million of zem, for no reason vatsoever. You deserve to rot in hell! *Guilty, guilty, guilty!*"

Hitler smiled back at this accuser, evidently pleased. "Two guilty," he said, "und von not guilty!"

We moved on to Ludvig (Von Beethoven), who stood up tall

and elegant in his black tails and white tie. He cleared his throat before writing down words to express himself. Once again, Tom translated, and his words came out into each of our respective native languages.

"Ludvig wrote this," Tom said. " 'Herr Hitler, my life has been devoted to music, pure and simple. I have lived in a different century than you. I don't understand who you are, or what you may have done, or why we are being asked to pass judgment on you. So I will abstain.' "

"Two guilty, und two not guilty!" Adolph yelled.

Next was Mike (Michelangelo), whose words in Italian again came out in each of our languages. "When I painted the Sistine Chapel," Mike said, "it was the first time that I was asked to paint the face and the body of God. Can you imagine that assignment? It was sacrilege! The Second Commandment states, *Do not make any graven images.* And there I was, every day, for four years, lying on my back on a scaffolding eighty feet high, making graven images of God!

"So now," he continued, "I'm asked to render judgment on another man, who has also sinned, almost every day of his later life. Only for him, it was the Sixth Commandment, *Thou shalt not kill!* So what am I supposed to do? *I'll tell you what I'll do! Both of us are as guilty as sin itself!*"

After another short silence, Adolph proclaimed, "Three guilty und two not guilty!"

Then Tom, the tall, fine-featured man known more for his writing than his speeches, stood up. "Gentlemen," he said in a high-pitched tone, "and ladies, I have two points of view here. On the one hand, I have spent most of my former life engaged in the pursuit of human rights. But there is a point beyond which no self-respecting man can go in the defense of liberty. As I understand the case before us, Mr. Hitler has crossed the line from fighting for a nation, or a reasonable cause, to the despicable practice of killing masses of people for no good reason. Such actions would normally deserve a guilty verdict.

"However," he continued, "the man standing before us today

is, to my mind, far apart in time and space, from the man who allegedly led Nazi Germany and persecuted Jews seventy years ago. I am not fully convinced that he is the same man in history that he claims to be, or that what all of us are experiencing now is not an illusion. I am not even convinced that *I* am real! Furthermore, this proceeding lacks any of the legal procedures with which I am acquainted. There is no real prosecutor, no defense attorney, nor even a book of rules to observe. Therefore, for all these reasons, I am compelled to abstain."

"Three guilty, und three not guilty!" came Adolph's triumphant voice.

The next to stand was Abe (Lincoln), already tall in stature, but eight inches taller as he donned his stovepipe hat. The craggy face stared out at the audience as he said, "Did you ever hear the story of the banker who offered to buy a horse from a farmer for $50?

"The farmer asked, 'What do you plan to do with him?'"

"The banker replied, 'Sell him to a renderer who will turn him into glue.'"

"'But this horse is a racer,' the farmer said. 'And besides, she's been my faithful companion for five years.'"

"The banker looked the farmer directly in the eye, and coldly replied, 'Mister, I don't let beauty get in the way of money.'"

"The farmer thought for a moment and then told the banker, 'Well Mister, I don't let money get in the way of beauty. No deal! And what's more, people like you, who destroy good things for no good reason, don't belong in banks. You belong behind bars.

"In this case, Adolf, like the banker, tried to mess this world up real good, and he too belongs behind bars. What's more, Adolph is white, male, and pretty well-educated, just like me. Makes me ashamed of my race, my gender, and my kind. Guilty as charged!"

"Four guilty, und three not guilty!" shouted Adolph, sounding pleased with each verdict, no matter what it was.

The next to stand was Eleanor (Roosevelt). Her white hair was tied in an elegant bun, and her blue eyes sparkled as she spoke in that painfully whiny voice.

"Friends," she said, "I know all too well the immense pain which so many millions have suffered as a result of Adolph's butchery. And I know that my husband, were he here today, would no doubt find him guilty and urge the death penalty. But I am not my husband. I have, some say, a more compassionate nature, and I can feel the extreme suffering in Adolph's life. I am going to say 'not guilty due to mental illness,' and recommend that he be kept in a facility like Rosewood for continued treatment."

"Four guilty, und four not guilty!" yelled Adolph.

Next to stand was Joan (of Arc). She simply said, in French (but somehow we could all understand), "Adolph, I love your passion and your desire to fight for a cause. Not guilty."

This made me want to puke. How could I have ever found her to be attractive? My brain must have disappeared— *kaput!*

"Four guilty, und five not guilty!" Adolph replied coldly.

Then the birthday boy, Jesus himself, stood up. "Like my friend, Sid," he said, "I cannot judge others. I can only show love and mercy. So I must abstain. But Adolph, please, *please* open up your heart. I know it's in there somewhere! That's all I ask."

A little softer, Adolph, stated, "Four guilty, und six not guilty."

At that moment, Ludwig stood up again. The words which he wrote down in German were translated dutifully by Tom: "After hearing everyone else, I would like to change my vote from not guilty to guilty."

"Zen five guilty und five not guilty," Adolph proclaimed. "You, Villiam, vill haf ze deciding vote."

Bill (Shakespeare) leaped onto the main table, dressed in his blue bard costume with the white plumed hat, and stated for all to hear,

My purpose, today—make you think and have fun.
In this first act, you'll see, whether justice is done.

193

But as for me, in the role of a juror,
I must self-recuse, from the trial of der Fuehrer.

Then Adolph screamed out, "*You can't do zis to me! Ve haf a shplit verdict, und ve need a decision. No, I need von more juror, und recusal ist not un option!*"

"Sir," replied Bill in a caustic tone. "You may be a fine orator, and a fair actor. But nobody writes my scripts but me! And I have no desire to play the part of a twenty-first century juror for your trial. If one more historical peer is what you desire, then you're stuck! Over! *Kaput! Get used to it! Shtuck!* After all the atrocities you appear to have committed, this problem is nothing!"

The mood in the room was turning sour, when suddenly a voice from behind the empty chair at the main table shouted, "*I'll serve!*"

It was a tall man with horn-rimmed glasses, a well-kept white beard, and a brown tie set off against a white shirt and brown suit. "Mein name," he said, "ist Sigmund Freud." (My first thought was that *I was getting tired of all these God-Damned German accents!*) "...und I vould be glad to serve as ze final juror in zis case."

"But you know *nodinkt* about me!" yelled an indignant ex-Chancellor.

"Belief me, Adolph," replied the world's greatest psychoanalyst, "I know more about you than *you* do!" Adolph was suddenly silent as Dr. Freud went on in German, (but for some reason the English speakers heard it come out in English).

"Ven you ver little, Adolph, your family lived for a time in ze town of Berchtesgaden, ver I also lived. I saw you crying almost every day after school from ze beatings of your fader. Your muder told me zat you had terrible nightmares. I asked her many times if I could treat you. But no, she vould haf none of it. So look vat happened to you! Mit no treatment, you vent on to murder millions of innocent people, und you became ze vorld's most hated man!"

Der Fuhrer asked softly, "So you knew mein mudder und fader?"

"Yavold, Adolph. I knew zem vell. Your mudder used to push you und your sister Paula on ze sving for hours. Und your fader, ven he vas sober, vould tell me how proud he vas of your persistence. He told me zat ven you vanted somezink, you vould never give up!"

"He nefer told *me* zat!" Adolph said angrily.

"Of course not," replied Freud. "He thought zat if he tolt you, zat vould make you veak. Und above all else, he vanted you to be shtrong. Yes, ze shtrongest man in ze world! *Vell, he got his God-Damned vish!*"

Adolph could not stand this any longer. He ran angrily toward Dr. Freud and tried to strike him. But our Rosewood staff was prepared, and they tackled him, held him in a position of restraint, and began to drag him off to the Quiet Room.

But Dr. Freud had other ideas. "*No!*" his voice rang out. "*Don't let him leaf zis room!* Let him shtay here, ver he und eferyvon can hear of ze *real* Adolph Hitler, vich has very little to do mit guns und nations, und everyting to do mit his fader, Alois!"

"*Nein!*" der Fueher screamed. "*You can't do zis! Ze trial ist over! Kaput! Now, everyvon, go home!*"

But Dr. Freud was not about to stop. "Adolph," he continued, "mein little Adolph. Do you remember ze day ven you ver valking home from school, und a big, blond, blue-eyed boy called Hans teased you about being Jewish?"

"*Nein!*" Adolph shouted. "*Nicht spreckenzie!*" (No, don't speak of that!)

"Adolph, zis is important! Zat big, blond, blue-eyed boy..."

"*Nein!*"

"Zat big, blond, blue-eyed boy, Hans, called you Adolphgoldfish, und you kept shcreaming at him zat you veren't Jewish. Und he insisted, saying zat your fader vas Jewish, und zat was Jewish enough to make you von too."

"*Nein!!*"

195

"You continued to tell him zat you veren't Jewish. But he said, 'Yes, you are, Adolphenshtein, *from your fader!* Vy else would you haf such a small, veak body, und such a gut brain. *From your fader,* Adolph. Little Jewish Adolphberg! *Your fader!* Und Hans laughed at you. You tried to hit him, but he vas shtronger, much shtronger. *Und I vas der*, Adolph! Looking out from mein open vindow from across ze shtreet! I saw it und heard it all! I vas *der!*"

Poor Adolph was now curled up in a fetal position, sobbing.

"Adolph, mein poor Adolph, I felt such pity for you! Und I knew zat I could help you. But no! Your mudder, und your fader too, both said no, zat you needed no help. *But you did need help!* Und zen you shouted something into ze air, vich I vill never forget. Do you recall vat it vas?"

Adolph rose from his fetal position, and yelled as loudly as he could, "*Mein sheister Jew fader! I shall kill you, und zen I shall kill all Jews, und zen I shall kill meinself! I shvear to almighty Hell!*"

With the room totally quiet, Adolph went back to a fetal position on the floor, tears streaming down his face.

The loyal Joan made an effort to go forth and help him, but she had trouble with her suit of armor again, and fell back down into her chair. Eventually it was Jesus, the birthday boy, who walked to the center of the room to comfort Adolph. The main lights of the room went out, and a single spotlight shone on the two of them, before fading into blackness.

There was scattered applause, as some in the audience suddenly remembered that this was just a play. And then Adolph, the actor, rose to his feet, bowed, and grinned. to a thunderous standing ovation. He waved to the celebrities at the main table, until they, too, all stood up and bowed, to more wild applause.

And then, one minute later, the same Adolph stood upon his chair, raised his right hand in the air in the traditional Nazi salute, and yelled out for all to hear, "*Heil Hitler!*"

Bewildered looks appeared on the faces of many people in the room, and silence returned.

CHAPTER TWENTY-FIVE

Ghosts

After Act One, I couldn't help but wonder how much of this play was scripted, and how much of it was extemporaneous. Everything had seemed so natural, with no clue of characters reading lines. But that was the job of the playwright and the actors. And at the end, the audience was thrilled by Adolph the actor, and then disgusted by what looked like Adolph the man. Which one had we just watched? We weren't sure.

A short time later, Bill (Shakespeare) walked once more to the center of this theater in the round and introduced Act Two:

America and liberty, land of opportunity,
  So proud and self-assured, for years!
But greed, guns and arrogance,
  Debt, and a lack of common sense
    May soon bring this land to tears.

The room went dark again. This time, after around fifteen seconds, the spotlight shone on a large bed in the center of the room. It looked like there was someone sleeping under the covers, but no sign as to who it was.

Suddenly, an enormous explosion nearby shook the building. *Kabooooom!*

There was a large flash of light, and from under the sheets came the cry of a man whose voice was familiar:

"*Stop!*" cried the voice of President Obama. "*Stop! Stop the drones attack! Now! This is President Obama! I'm your Commander-in-Chief! Stop the drones! I order you! Now!*"

But the explosions kept coming, from all sides.
Ka-booom! Kabbooomm! Kabbooooom!

"*Stop! Stop! I order you, NOW!*" he yelled, to no avail.

Then a soldier dressed in a Civil War Union uniform came into the "bedroom." He had a black beard, and was holding a rifle.

"*Don't shoot!*" yelled the President. "This is your Commander-in-Chief, President Barack Obama. And I order you not to shoot!"

The soldier stood in front of the president and looked at him.

"Who are you?" asked the president, shaking.

"I," the soldier replied, this time in clear English, "am the Ghost of War. I have come to tell you and all America that your fightin' ways are causin' your demise."

A closer look at the face revealed that it was Abraham Lincoln. I looked over at Lincoln's seat and noticed that he was missing. So this was our own Honest Abe, playing himself!

"Mr. Lincoln," replied Obama, "I know that you presided over our country's most terrible war. And I know that you lived in the White House, in the bedroom next to ours. But I never expected to meet you in person."

"Mr. President," Lincoln replied, "three times in the last fifty years, America has sent more than one hundred thousand soldiers into battle in Asian countries where its soldiers couldn't even speak the language. Your defense budget exceeds those of the next ten countries combined. America still has large bases in eleven other countries, and it accounts for half of the weapons sales on the planet. And here at home anyone can buy automatic weapons. This is all idiocy!"

"But Mr. Lincoln," Obama protested, "I just got our troops out of Iraq, and I'm doing what I can to get our troops out of Afghanistan. And I'm trying to cut the defense budget. I'm doing exactly what you suggest!"

But the Ghost of War had disappeared.

*****

After another minute of blackness, the spotlight shone again on the presidential bed. This time the president's head was outside the covers, and he was sitting upright, alone.

Suddenly a tapping could be heard at one of the windows of our cafeteria. The face of a man appeared in it. It was dark-skinned, with disheveled hair, and had an insistent expression.

"Psst, Barack," the voice said in a whisper. "Over here!"

"What the devil?" cried the president. "Who's there?"

"Hey Barack!" called the voice again. "Let me in! It's me! Madison!"

"Madison?" The president looked at the man's face in the window, and recognized him instantly. Then, with a grin, the President opened the window and let the stranger in.

"Madison Hemings!" said the president. "What in hell are *you* doing here? Why, I haven't seen you since law school! And why are you dressed in rags? Hey buddy, wha-sup?"

The two men fist-pumped and held each other in smiles and a long embrace. The audience could see that Madison Hemings, a black man, looked like a dark-skinned Thomas Jefferson. He was dressed in torn brown rags, but had Tom's delicate features and even a little of his squeaky voice. I looked at the empty seat where Tom had been sitting and realized that this was him. The man who was so well-known in the fields of architecture, horticulture. music, literature, science, philosophy, etc, was now an actor playing the part of a black member of his own family!

"Madison, you could have been shot coming through the window like that! And probably should have been!"

"Barack, brother," replied Madison with an easy smile. "Dis ain't no different from de days of my black-assed ancestor by de same name. Only dat nigger had it much worse than dis nigger! Back den dey strung us up on trees. Now dey just buzz us in de 'lectric chair!"

"Well tell me, bro, whas happenin'? Why you here?" Both men were affecting an old Negro accent—a kind of bonding which had developed over their time in law school.

"I's here 'cause I need you to change."

"Change? Whatchu mean change, brother? I's doing de best I can!"

"No you ain't!"

"Yes, I is!"

"No you ain't!"

"Yes, I is! Do you think it's easy bein' a black-ass President?"

"No, but listen up..."

"Okay, but tell me first. How's your mother?"

"Sallie? Sallie's dyin' of AIDS on a grate two blocks from here, as we speak. And that's the truth! So help me God!" The playful accent ceased.

"Dying? On a grate? What happened to Sallie's good health, and her nice home?"

"Gone, *gone!* First she got laid off her teaching job. Then she got desperate for money and tried hooking to pay the rent. Then she got sick and couldn't pay for doctors or meds. And then she got more sick. At first she didn't tell me, but then I found out and dropped out of my law practice to try to help her. *Barack, I couldn't stand it!* You remember Sallie! One of the nicest, hardest-working people you'll ever meet, and then all this happened! *Barack, I couldn't stand it!* I tried gettin' another job to help her. But I too got depressed and couldn't hold it down! So there we were—the two of us—fighting pimps and police and drug dealers and rain and sleet and all— just to survive! Barack, you can't imagine..."

Madison collapsed in Barack's arms and sobbed. Neither said anything for a while.

Then the President said, "Madison, my brother, what about your father? Maybe he could help."

"Tom?" said Madison. "Help? No way! He's a white boy, living it up in a white man's world! He's with his white family in a mansion down in Florida. Goldman Sachs is paying him $2 million a year just to sit there on his white ass, building more rooms and swimming pools! That's what he's doing! Two million a year! Another God-Damned Monticello! Just like the old Tom! And here's the new Tom's mama sleepin' on a grate, and she's dyin' of *AIDS! Shit!* He knows where we are! He knows my mother's condition! I keep sending him letters, hoping he'll change his mind. But no! He won't even acknowledge that we're kin! Just like the old Tom! *The old motherfuckin' Thomas Jefferson!* My dad, like the old Tom, can't speak the truth because he'd lose too fuckin' much! It's all the same, Barack! Just like two hundred years ago! *It's all the same!*"

"So what can I do?"

"Barack, first I want you to help Sallie by bringing her and me into your Lincoln bedroom. Just for a few months, until she can get some medical help and get back on her feet. Then I want you to open up the White House lawn to homeless people, maybe just a few hundred, so they don't have to sleep no more on grates and such. And then I want you to pay 50% tax on your income, just like in your speeches. Brother, you can't be just talkin' the talk. You gotta walk the walk!"

"But Madison, I can't do *any* of these things! This is the *White House!* It's all about national security! And I can't start giving away money! I've got Sasha and Malia to think about. They'll be going to college soon, and..."

But the Ghost of Greed had vanished.

*****

Again the cafeteria lay in darkness for what seemed like a long time. Eventually a spotlight lit up President Obama, once again lying in bed, wide awake this time, and searching for the next ghostly creature, as in Dickens' story, *The Christmas Carol.*

This time it was more of an alien, a green alien, which floated down from the cafeteria's high ceiling. The figure was covered in a thin sheen which was transparent and illuminated no flesh, but the face was quite clear. It belonged to none other than Eleanor Roosevelt!

After clearing her throat, she said, "Mr. President, may I call you 'Barack'?" It was another squeaky voice, and the president gazed up at her in astonishment.

"Yes, of course, Mrs. Roosevelt. I have always been one of your greatest admirers."

The green ghostly image of Eleanor Roosevelt looked down at the current President. "Barack," she said, "I too, am one of *your* greatest admirers. So many wonderful things you have done."

"Thank you," replied the president in a soft tone. "May I ask what brings you here, in the middle of the night?"

"Yes, of course," she answered. "I have just one small request."

"Yes?"

"I want you to give up your citizenship."

"*What?* But I'm President of the United States! I'm its leader!"

"I know, Barack, and that's why you're the perfect one to do it. Nationalism is one of the two most destructive forces in our world today."

"What's the other?"

"Religion, but I don't think you can do much about that."

"So what do you expect me to do after I renounce my country?"

"I want you to start an organization called Planet Earth United. It would offer equal membership to every person on our planet, and a view of our planet that transcends national politics. It would include something like the Universal Declaration of Human Rights, and it would promote peace and freedom for all peoples."

"But we already have a United Nations. Why wouldn't the new organization be a part of that?"

"Because the United Nations is still stuck in its 1940s mode, and controlled by the Big Five powers of that era. We need something modern, and something without nations."

"Mrs. Roosevelt, if I did that, I would lose my base here in America. My countrymen would shun me as a pariah, and I would lose my proud legacy in American history!"

But the Ghost of Unity was gone.

CHAPTER TWENTY-SIX

Pilgrims

As the lights came on for the Third Act, Bill leaped onto the stage and bellowed out the following:

Religions, all, can serve us well,
Can bring us love, but also Hell
So can these leaders all unite
In common purpose, or will they fight?

A man in an orange robe was sitting alone on a yellow pillow, elevated three feet above the cafeteria floor, with no visible means of support. His arms were resting on his knees, and his legs were crossed and comfortable in the traditional lotus position.

"Hey Sid!" The impassioned voice from offstage was unmistakable. It was Jesus. He ran into the spotlight, looked at Buddha, and said, "So there you are."

"Yes, my friend. I'm never far away. What's on your mind?"

"I've got an idea!"

"Yes? Please tell me."

"Why don't you and I join together and preach tolerance throughout the world? This could be the most powerful force for peace and love our planet has ever known!" There was great excitement in his voice.

Buddha smiled and looked at Jesus for a moment. "My good friend," he said, "your intentions seem honorable, and I would enjoy spending time with you on such a mission. But I must warn you against unrealistic expectations."

"What do you mean?"

"A thousand things could happen. For example, a group of fanatics could crucify you, like the last time. Or a bomb could take the lives of both of us. Or maybe no one would believe that we were who we said we were. After all, this coming-back-from-the-dead business stretches the imagination."

"But don't you think this is worth a chance? Life is full of risks, and we can't let that stop us from doing what we think is right. I think you call that *dharma*."

"Well, I tell you what. If you can find Moses and Mohammed and get them to join us on such a trip, I'll be glad to join you."

"How can I do that? Neither of them is a Rosewood resident, and we've already reached our limit of twelve."

"Oh Jesus, sometimes you are so naive."

With this, Buddha closed his eyes and went into a trance. Thunder and lightning struck his disappearing body, and soon, in his place, standing tall with a black beard, black robe and fire in his eyes, was a magnificent figure which, to all of us, looked and felt a lot like the messenger, Mohammed.

The first words out of Mohammed's mouth were in Arabic. Then he spoke out in fluent English, "Where am I, when is this time, and what is happening to me?"

Noticing Jesus in front of him, he said, "Good sir, my mind seems to be in disarray. Can you help answer some of these questions?"

"Yes," replied Jesus calmly. "It appears that both of us have been brought back from the dead for some purpose. The year is 2012, dating from the approximate time of my birth."

"And who are you?"

"My name is Jesus of Nazareth. You may recall references to me in your *Qu'ran*. We are both of Jewish heritage and descendants of Abraham."

"Jesus?" The mighty messenger of Allah looked at the man before him and smirked. "Jesus? You claim to be Jesus of Nazareth? Son of Mary and Joseph?"

He gave a mighty laugh. "You're mad. The real Jesus died centuries before I was born. As the story goes, he was reborn once, and now you expect me to believe that he was reborn again, and that you are him?"

"Yes, just as you too were reborn after descending into Heaven from the Dome of the Rock, and have now been reborn again, inexplicably, after your death in Medina."

"Jesus, you keep using the calendar which begins with the year of your birth. What arrogance! Why don't we start the calendar on the year of the *Hegira*, and say that you were born in the year 632 B.H.—before the Hegira?"

"Suit yourself," Jesus answered. "I have little interest in dates. My real question to you is this: 'Would you be willing to join me on a journey to preach love and tolerance throughout the world?' It appears that some of our followers are fighting each other in our names, and that we may be able to dissuade them from this folly."

"Ha!" Mohammed replied in a cynical tone. "Even if you were Jesus, which seems preposterous, what makes you think we could get along with each other? Have you ever read the *Qu'ran*?"

"No. I don't know how to read Arabic. How do you expect people to understand the world of Allah, when you refuse to allow the *Qu'ran* to be translated into other languages?"

Upon hearing this criticism, Mohammed drew his bejeweled sword from its scabbard. "Listen, Jesus, or whoever you are! Insulting me, the *Qu'ran* and Allah all at once would gain most people an immediate place in Hell. One more remark like that, and I swear by all that is holy in Islam that you, or whomever you claim to be, will meet an instant death, in which case you would have to, once more, test your powers of arising from the dead."

"I'm very sorry," Jesus replied in a soft tone. "I meant no insult. But the truth is that you, I, and the prophet Moses are all of one family, whether or not our Lord is called 'Allah' or 'Jehovah.' We have much more in common than..."

At this point, there was another mighty clash of thunder and a flash of lightning, as a third character appeared on stage.

"Speak for yourself, Jesus!" yelled a large, gray-robed, barrel-chested man with enormous biceps.

"And who might you be, to interrupt us in such a manner?" challenged an angry Mohammed.

"My name is Moses," said the newly-arrived stranger. "And I can assure you that there is only one Chosen People on this planet, and that they are god-fearing Jews. The word of God cannot be found in either the *Qu'ran* or the *New Testament*, but only in the five books of the *Torah*. And it appears that neither of you have learned this as yet."

Once again, Mohammed raised his sword, and this time he proceeded to bring it down on the man before him, Moses. But just before the sword was about to strike Moses' head, the sword turned into a cobra, which coiled on the floor next to Mohammed and threatened to strike him.

Mohammed's reaction was to laugh heartily. He said, "Moses, you did this once before to an Egyptian Pharaoh, and now again to me. I will no longer treat you as an enemy to be slain. But what a curious presence—the three of us together, outside of normal time."

"Correction!" boomed a voice from behind the three holy men, "we are not three, but four!" The voice was that of Buddha, who was once more comfortably seated on a yellow pillow a short distance away.

"And who, in the name of Allah, are you?" Mohammed shouted.

"My name is Siddhartha Gautama, otherwise known as Buddha. I have no personified God to offer you. But I do have a spiritual nature, and like the three of you, a considerable following amongst some of the people here on Earth."

This was followed by silence as the four holy men gazed back and forth at each other, in an awkward manner.

Jesus broke the silence. "My good friends," he said, "may I remind you that we have all been physically transformed into the year 2012, and that many of our followers appear to be at war with each other. There are Israeli Jews against Palestinian Muslims, Afghan Muslims against Christian Americans, and Iraqi Shi-ites against Iraqi Sunnis, just for a start. There is much work to be done. So if we can all, somehow, unite..."

"*Unite?*" Mohammed cried out. "How could I unite with a Christian, a Jew, and a god-knows-what? That would betray my total commitment to Allah, the only Lord of us all. Even if you do appear to be good men, we have *no common ground!*" He

209

yelled these last words in a defiant tone, as if he wanted Allah Himself to hear them.

Poor Jesus hung his head for a few seconds, raised it, and replied, "We have love, tolerance and good will towards all. Mohammed, I've heard that the word which appears more than any other in the *Qu'ran* is *mercy!* Surely these must be common threads for us all. And if not, then let us consider *family*. All but one of us are descendants of Abraham. And if Abraham were here, he would surely want us to come together."

The four holy men looked around, half expecting Abraham himself to appear. But he didn't.

Moses turned to Buddha and said, "Siddhartha, you're the outsider here. What are your thoughts about this pilgrimage which Jesus has proposed?"

Buddha, with his rotund figure resting in total calm on his little white pillow, answered, "The truth is that I have no preferences. The world is unfolding just as it should. And I will accept any outcome, whether it be unity, no unity, or something else."

"But don't you *care?*" said Jesus, in a strident tone. "The people on Earth have nuclear weapons now, which could destroy everything which our Lord has created. Don't you care *at all* about this?"

Jesus, Moses, and Mohammed looked at Buddha, who smiled at them while remaining totally calm. "Yes," he said, "and no. Yes, I feel compassion for all living things, human and other. And yes, I would be glad to join the three of you on such a trip—if you could all get along. And no, I feel no attachment to the outcome of such a mission. Whatever will be, will be."

Once again there was silence. The children of Abraham appeared to be clueless to the total acceptance value which Buddha was extolling.

"Well, Moses," said Jesus, "How about you? Would you be willing to join Siddhartha and me on a good will tour, preaching peace and love to people of all faiths?"

"Frankly," replied Moses, "I have little interest in the non-Jews of this world. I've had my hands full just trying to keep my people following the Ten Commandments handed down to me, personally, by our god."

"But Moses," Jesus persisted, "aren't love and tolerance of all people a part of the Ten Commandments and your religion?"

"That's a good question," replied Moses. "You know, to be perfectly honest, I think we are commanded to love the Lord, and to honor our parents, but not to love everyone. We're certainly not expected to love our enemies. You won't find that in our scripture."

"Moses," Jesus continued, "We have a situation now in the Middle East where a hatred of Israel and Judaism is threatening to extinguish not only your religion, but the whole planet. Wouldn't you like to join Buddha and me in trying to bring these sides together and make peace?"

"I suppose I could do that," he answered. "But I couldn't promise anything specific in advance. After all, my only real allegiance is to the protection and prosperity of my own people."

"Then it's settled," Jesus replied, "You, Siddhartha, and I have agreed to go together on a pilgrimage for peace."

Again silence.

"So, Mohammed," Jesus said, "what would it take for you to join us?"

"First of all," Mohammed replied, "credibility. At this point we are just four crazy characters meeting in a dining hall with delusions that we are holy. And of course, there is the little fact that all of us have been dead for centuries. Why do you think anyone would believe this ridiculous story?"

"Miracles," Jesus replied. "Each of us, I believe, is capable of performing supernatural acts, and this alone should persuade many disbelievers."

"Nonsense," said Mohammed. "Miracles like turning swords into snakes can be easily performed by the real magicians of this day. But such miracles give no proof as to who we are, or how we may have arrived in this age."

"Well, OK, some people would believe that we are whom we claim to be, and some wouldn't. But that's no reason for not trying to bring more peace to the world."

"All right, let's say we get past this problem of credibility. Then how do we preach our separate doctrines? So I go out and tell my followers about Allah and the *Qu'ran*, You preach about your Lord and the *New Testament*, Moses preaches about Jehovah and the *Torah*, and Buddha preaches about god-knows-what. This doesn't make sense. There's almost nothing that we can agree on."

"How about the killing of innocent people?" replied Jesus. "Surely you could condemn Al Queda for their attack on the innocent people in the New York World Trade Center. That was clearly wrong."

"Nonsense!" Mohammed replied. "Do you recall the events that led up to this action?"

"Nothing can excuse what they did," Jesus replied.

"How about the building of a Christian military base in Rhiyad, inside the holy land of Saudi Arabia? And how about decades of America's total support for Israel, despite their many aggressions against Palestinians? Are you so ignorant as to not be aware of this history?"

"No, of course not," Jesus blustered. "But that doesn't excuse such a monstrous attack on innocent people in New York City!"

"Well then, what excuse do you have for the American invasion and occupation of Iraq and Afghanistan? These are Moslem countries, and your Christian armies are killing innocent Moslems in Afghanistan as we speak! Do you not call this monstrous? How would you answer such protests of Moslems on a world-wide tour? Do you support these wars by your own followers, or are you against them?"

"I am against them."

"Good. So how do you expect your Christian American leaders will react to your criticism of their policies? Do you think they will suddenly take all their soldiers out of Afghanistan? No way! You're a dreamer, Jesus! Your followers never did listen to your pacifist views, and they're not about to start now! This pilgrimage you propose is totally ill-conceived!"

"I'd like to interject something here," said Moses.

"During my life, mostly in Egypt, I never killed anyone or even had to wear a sword. But I didn't need to. The Lord did that for me—by smiting Egyptians, bad-behaving Jews, and others who stood in the way of His chosen people. Yes, one of the Ten Commandments was *Thou Shalt Not Kill*. But the Lord, by His actions, helped us fight enemies in just wars. Judaism is not pacifist, and so we have a split here between Islam, Judaism, and militant Christianity on the one hand, and pure Christianity and Buddhism on the other. In a world torn by religious wars, it's hard to see the common ground."

Jesus was clearly flustered.

Buddha re-entered the conversation. "Let us not forget," he said, "that we are all human, or at least part human. And that the three of you are family, direct descendants of Abraham. Should you let your respective religious views tear you apart? Is this the true spirit of your beliefs, or of your god? I don't think so. I further believe that if it were possible for the four of us to live in harmony, and demonstrate that harmony to others on this planet, that we could steer today's people away from such unnecessary wars. It would be a major challenge for all four of us. But as Jesus has said, why not give it a try? Mohammed, I see this as a major test of your tolerance. Will you join Jesus, Moses, and I, and acknowledge our commonality, or are you so committed to the separateness of Islam that there is no room in it for people with other points of view?"

There was another period of silence, in which Mohammed was struggling to find an answer. Then, at last, he said, "Allah has always shown mercy to others outside of his faith. Joining the three of you feels better than standing in opposition."

"So it's settled, then," replied Jesus. "We will make the necessary arrangements as soon as possible."

"*Who* will?" Moses replied. "Remember that we are all perceived to be mad. We will need at least one guide who can work with each of us, difficult as this may be."

213

At this point I rose from my seat in the audience and yelled, *"How about me? I'll volunteer! I'm very qualified, and I'll be glad do it!"*

From my left came another voice, that of Bertie. "Patrick," he said, "don't be an idiot! This is a play, not reality. So just sit down and enjoy the show!"

"Mr. Wells," Jesus said to Bertie, "this may appear to be a scripted play to you, but I couldn't be more serious. I have every intention of making such a peace pilgrimage, even if it leads to my second crucifixion. And I, for one, welcome Patrick's interest, and his participation."

Another voice, a high-pitched female one, yelled from the right of me, "Boys, boys! Once again, you have succeeded in shutting out the ladies from an important endeavor."

It was Eleanor. "If you're going to tour the world for peace, then you absolutely need to have at least one female along for the ride. And my credentials, as one of the founders of the United Nations, should speak for themselves. I insist upon joining you, and that's that!"

Jesus said, "Yes, of course."

Moses and Mohammed squirmed a little, but there was no objection.

"And Sigmund and I," said Al, "need to join you because you need more Jews."

"And Abe and I," said Tom, "need to join you because you need more Christian Americans."

And so it went. Ludwig could not bear to leave behind his new "family." Joan could not bear to leave Eleanor behind, and Mike had bonded with Ludwig. Bertie could not bear to miss all the excitement, and that left Adolph.

"Ah *hah!*" Adolph yelled, "Vould you leave behint poor little me just because I'm a Nazi? Are you all so *prejudiced?* Vat about zes principles of *equality*? Am I not *human* enough for you? After all, I hav not yet been found guilty! Ah *hah!* So please, pretty please, vould you let me come along too? Pretty please, mit cream und sugar…"

Silence.

"How about *zis*?" Adolph continued, "How about if I come in disguise, und tell no one who I really am. Zey vould never guess! Ah *hah!* I vould be qvuiet as a mouse."

More silence.

The lights in the room went out and all was dark.

When the lights came on again, all the characters in the three-act play were bowing, and we started clapping. A great performance, but no resolution! How weird! So unlike Bill's other plays.

CHAPTER TWENTY-SEVEN

The Dance

"Let's dance!"

The speaker was the little girl in the wheelchair, who had moved to the center of the room.

After the *sturm und drang* of Bill's play, this was a welcome change of mood. Ludwig raised his baton, and the Auburn Symphony Orchestra began to play an inspired version of Bach's *Brandenburg Concerto #3*.

The first one to get up and dance was my own little Brigit, who never could keep still when bouncy music was playing. Oblivious to everyone else in the cafeteria, and to everything else that might have been happening, she moved in delightful circles, arms swaying above her head, eyes beaming as if moved by God Himself, or Herself, or who knows, or cares? Her little body was full of grace, innocence and beauty. Joining her in the center of the room was little Peter, the son of Rich Barton, the dwarf. Then came Sasha and Malia Obama. Children all, the next generation—the future.

Next to enter the dance floor were Tom and Eleanor, who began doing a dance from the 18th Century. The volume of the concerto grew louder, and more people came out to dance.

After unveiling his special sculpture—an exquisite white marble statue of the little girl in the wheelchair, Mike went across the room to ask Tawny to be his partner; and a radiance came to her eyes that I had never seen before. Adolph asked his precious Joan to dance, and she took off her armor and, in flowing garments of the 14th century, stepped nimbly with him to the center of the floor. As more male Rosewood residents at the head table came forward, the consideration of gender-matching was thrown to the winds. Einstein danced with Freud, Wells with Abe Lincoln, and Jesus with Buddha. Moses asked Mohammed to dance. After some hesitation, Mohammed came to the floor, linked arms with Moses, and they twirled together with broad smiles and laughter. Wow!

As the music played on, the rest of us could hardly sit still. President and Mrs. Obama, the Arab family, the Bartons, the staffers, and even Fred Smedley, stepped forward. As I joined them, I noticed that the dancers had formed two concentric circles, going in opposing directions, like square dancers doing an *a-la-main right* and *a-la-main left*. As the tune changed to Beethoven's own *Ode de Joy*, the little girl lifted her tiny body out of the wheelchair and spun above us like a whirling dervish before floating down to join the rest of us in the circle dance. The feeling was one of pure joy. No ego. No prejudice. Nothing negative. Just joy!

We went outside to witness a gorgeous sunset, and then a clear, starry night. The temperature was warm, and the music kept playing, on and on, and it was all deliriously happy. The dance moved on to many different rhythms and cultures. There were drumbeats from Africa, sitars from India, and flutes from the Peruvian Andes. A flamenco guitar, a Russian balalaika, and a New Zealand didgeridoo. Then came Jesus doing impersonations of Louis Armstrong, Frank Sinatra, and Garth Brooks. And Buddha doing His impersonations of Elvis, Jay-Z and Beyoncé.

Over time, we became a little tired, and it would have been nice for the evening to end with all of us just falling asleep on the ground.

But such was not to be.

CHAPTER TWENTY-EIGHT

The Girl

"Now," said the little girl, in the middle of our nighttime spree, "let us return to our seats." She led us back to our chairs in the cafeteria, like schoolchildren being led back into the classroom by their teacher after recess. With such powerful people as Jesus, Buddha, Mohammed, Moses and Obama in our group, there was no question at this moment as to who was in charge.

"So now," she said to us all, "let me describe my view of the big picture."

All was quiet in the room. The greatest collection of minds in history was quiet, and listening.

"As mentioned during my last visit," she said, "I am a being from another universe. I have told you some of my story before, and it was chronicled in Rich Barton's book, *Another Messiah.* But here is a part of it again, for those of you who may not be familiar with my mission."

She paused.

"For many years, I have been studying humankind's life on what you call Planet Earth. And I have come to love you."

Another pause.

"I can see that, if left alone, you are likely to destroy yourselves and much of life as you know it on Earth within the next one hundred years."

Pause.

"On my first visit," she continued, "I tried to help your people in various ways, by stopping some of the violence, helping you with some social problems, and cleaning up some of your environment."

Pause.

"On this current visit, I brought back from the dead some of the most interesting people in your planet's history."

Pause.

"The question you may be asking now is 'Why?'"

Pause. (We were glued to every word.)

"It was my original intention to have you bond here at Rosewood, before bringing you back to my home, far away."

Pause.

"However, Jesus has come up with an interesting suggestion: that your religious leaders make a pilgrimage for peace. Then others here decided that they would like to join them on this pilgrimage."

Pause.

"I am considering this idea now, and I'd like to hear more of your thoughts."

She stopped talking and waited for us to respond. Bill (Shakespeare) was the first to speak.

"I like Jesus' idea," he said, "but I think it would be dangerous to do it in a straightforward manner. As mentioned earlier, if we pretended to be ourselves coming back from the dead, we would likely arouse the wrath of non-believers. The whole thing could turn violent before it even started. Therefore I propose that we pose as actors playing the roles of famous people. That way, there could be a place even for Adolph. We could call ourselves *The Rosewood Players*. And since President Obama is here now and has some understanding as to who we are, the United States military wouldn't feel threatened. "

"Yes," was the current president's simple reply.

"I like the idea," said Bertie. "But I think our religious leaders had better be prepared for some big questions. With Jesus, they will want to know his ideas on subjects like abortion, birth control, and gay marriage, just for a start."

"I would need to prepare for these things," Jesus said, "but it could be done."

"Moses," said Al, "How would you reconcile the cause of your Chosen People, with the cause of all humankind?"

The purveyor of the Ten Commandments said, "I too think that this could be done. After all, we don't ask others to convert to Judaism. We leave them in peace to follow their own spiritual paths. Co-existence must be the common principle, for the survival of us all."

"And you, Mohammed," said Tom, "how would you deal with fanatic Muslims, such as those in Al Qaeda? Or those who want to use Sharia law to stone to death women who are accused of being unfaithful? Or who want to kill anyone making any portrayal of yourself? You know you couldn't act as yourself in a play without being instantly mobbed and killed. Even poor Patrick, who is writing his book, and journalist Fred Smedley—even they would be placing themselves at enormous risk. And how would you deal with the issue of *fatwa*? So many questions, Mohammed!"

Mohammed grinned at everyone. "Ah, my friends," he said, "I think, for this kind of preparation, I would need to return to my cave outside Mecca, and speak once again to my Lord, Allah."

Standing up tall, once again, was "Honest Abe," who asked this last question of the evening, "Ma'am," he said, addressing the little girl, "pardon my not knowing your name, so I'll just call you 'Ma'am'… I have another idea. Having had some experience in matters relating to personal security, I wonder if you, with your powers, might not take over the job of protecting us against those who might desire to do us harm. Just a thought."

After a pause, the little girl looked at Lincoln and said, "Abraham, this is a good idea. But I suspect that its implementation would be difficult—even for me." This requires more thought.

"So many good questions," she continued, "and good ideas! Why don't we just retire now, get a good night's sleep, and meet again here in the morning, over breakfast."

###

Acknowledgments

To my wife Elsa and our son Austin, who have been loving and understanding through another of my creative ventures;

To Jane Roach, my partner and angel at Sierra Dreams Press

To Fred Buechner, my religion teacher at Exeter, who opened up my spiritual mind;

To Mac Runyan, my advisor at U.C. Berkeley, with whom I share a fascination with life stories and in particular the life of Adolph Hitler;

To Walter Klein and Madonna Anglin, great editors and proof-readers;

To my friends at the center where I work, all of whom are struggling with, or helping others struggle with, such challenges as addiction, homelessness and mental illness;

And to all those on our planet who are caught in the grip of hunger, injustice, pestilence, poverty or war, and who might benefit from a major paradigm shift such as the one described in this novel.

Sierra Dreams Press

Sierra Dreams Press was founded by Stuart Rawlings and Jane Roach in 2005, with the purpose of publishing some of Stuart's written and musical works, and the works of others as well. Its website now offers these items:

Books
Now available in paperback, e-book and audiobook formats

Another Messiah (novel written in 2005)
Delusions (sequel written in 2012)
The God Child (sequel written in 2019)

My Favorite Quotations, Volumes 1-8 (1971, 1976, 1981, 1986, 1991, 1998, 2007 and 2018)
Good Soldier Wolf (by Jiri Wolf and SR, 1992)
IVS Experiences: from Algeria to Viet Nam (Edited by SR, 1992)
Auburn's Creative People (2), by SR and Jane Roach (2007 and 2008)
Love Interrupted, Lila Guerrero (Autobiography, 2000)
*The Monster in the Cave, (*children's book by Austin and Stuart Rawlings, 2009)

CDs

Memories (CD of 26 songs performed by SR)

Life is a Treasure (CD of 20 songs written and performed by SR)

Christmas in Auburn (CD of 20 songs performed   by SR and the Auburnaires, 2008)

Auburn, U.S.A. (CD of 20 songs performed by SR and the Auburnaires, 2005)

Videos

(look in YouTube under Stuart Rawlings)

I Like Junk Food, by SR and David Anastasiou, 2011

Austin's Dream, by SR and David Anastasiou, 2010

Lucky Man, by SR and the Auburnaires, 2010

All the books and CDs are available through:
Sierra Dreams Press
15200 Wild Oak Lane
Auburn, CA 95603
(530) 878-8831
www.sierradreamspress.com
stuartrawlings@hughes.net

"Life is precious, and there is no time to lose."